DRUMS THUNDERED IN MY EARS.

Buli's body swayed in rhythm to their beats, as though he and the drums were one and the same. When the drums reached a crescendo, he turned in my direction and thrust a ring at me. It bore the symbol of a skull.

I raised my hand, and he slipped the ring onto my finger. It fit perfectly. As I stared at the ring, it began to glow. Rays of light shot out of it. I knew—without knowing why—that I was no longer Kit Walker, that I was now someone much different and more powerful. I squeezed my eyes shut and saw, in the shadows and tendrils of light, the new name I would take.

From this time on, I would be known as the Phantom.

THE PHANTOM

A novel by Rob MacGregor
Based on the screenplay written by Jeffrey Boam
Based on the characters created by Lee Falk

AVON BOOKS ◆ NEW YORK

THE PHANTOM is an original publication of Avon Books. This work has never before appeared in book form. This work is a novel by Rob MacGregor based on a screenplay by Jeffrey Boam, based on the characters created by Lee Falk. Any similarity to actual persons or events is purely coincidental.

AVON BOOKS
A division of
The Hearst Corporation
1350 Avenue of the Americas
New York, New York 10019

Copyright © 1996 by King Features Syndicate, Inc./Paramount Pictures Corporation
Published by arrangement with King Features Syndicate, Inc./Paramount Pictures Corporation
Library of Congress Catalog Card Number: 96-96130
ISBN: 0-380-78887-X

First Avon Books Printing: June 1996

AVON TRADEMARK REG. U.S. PAT. OFF. AND IN OTHER COUNTRIES, MARCA REGIS-
TRADA, HECHO EN U.S.A.

Printed in the U.S.A.

RA   10   9   8   7   6   5   4   3   2   1

FROM THE CHRONICLES:
HOW IT ALL BEGAN

O

ONE

June 1533
The Sea of Bangalla

For the past two days, I had felt as if we were being watched. It was a ridiculous feeling—that was what I kept telling myself. After all, we were on the open ocean and there had been no land sighted since we'd left an isolated tropical island five days ago. There had been only the sea—an endless blue as vast as the sky itself.

Nevertheless, the feeling had intensified, and now one of my father's crew had spotted a ship on the horizon that was growing quickly in size. I tried not to show any fear. The son of the captain was expected to be as brave as the captain himself. I was one of the measurements the crew used to gauge my father's moods. If I showed fear, they would assume my father was also afraid. It didn't matter if it wasn't an accurate reflection; that was simply how it was.

I knew we were no match for the fierce bands of pirates who roamed these seas off the coast of Bangalla. They were among the most dreaded pirates on all the seas. Usually they killed the crew, ransacked the ship, and then sank it.

Our ship wasn't outfitted with even a single cannon. Instead of weapons, the cargo hold was packed with hammers, saws, knives, and other steel tools and utensils, which were destined for a settlement near the Cape of Good Hope. We also carried bales of raw wool and bundles of woolen goods, including winter undergarments and heavy coats.

I hoped that if the pirates caught us, they wouldn't be interested in our cargo and would let us go. But I had the feeling it wouldn't work out that way.

We weren't even supposed to be anywhere near the Bangalla coast, but we'd been blown far off course by a tremendous storm. Several of the crew had been washed overboard, we had sustained damage to the ship, and were indeed fortunate that our merchant vessel was still afloat.

After the storm, we'd come upon the island and spent two weeks there resting and making repairs to the ship. The natives on the island were friendly, and we traded fresh food and water for some of our merchandise. They liked the tools, but didn't have much use for the clothing. Still, some of the more adventurous natives were soon parading around in their loin cloths with wool scarfs around their necks or heads and long underwear wrapped around their shoulders.

Truly, the island was a pleasant enough place and the people were handsome and, like I said, friendly, so friendly, in fact, some of the crew members were courting the attractive young women and perhaps hoping that we would stay there. We wouldn't be the first.

From a shipwrecked sailor named Sam, we'd found out that we had been blown right through the dangerous seas controlled by the notorious Bangalla pirates, and that to return to our course, we would need to sail through those waters again. The sailor, who had three native wives and a dozen children, had no interest in joining us and suggested that we join him. Challenging the fierce Bangalla pirates was a lost cause, he'd said.

But my father, who was truly a fearless man, wasn't going to be stopped by a few pirates. At my age, he had been a cabin boy on Columbus's third journey to the New World. Nothing, he claimed, could equal that trip in danger. Besides, as he told the crew, he felt sure we would never encounter the pirates.

I was the eldest of five children, and at age ten, this was my first voyage. I trusted my father's judgment, of course. I would do whatever he wanted. At the same time, I was curious about the Bangalla pirates and wanted to know more about them.

I'd become acquainted with one of the shipwrecked sailor's sons, who was a year or two younger than I was. He told me the strangest story I'd ever heard—that the Bangallans had navigators who could actually leave their bodies and fly like frigate birds over the seas in search of ships to pillage. When they returned to their bodies, they knew exactly where to find their floating prey. I had never heard of such magic and asked my father if he thought it was true.

He just laughed, naturally, and said it was a native superstition; nothing for us to worry about. He assured me we would sail soon and pass quickly through the pirate waters and continue our journey. We would make our delivery, and before I knew it, I would be home telling exotic tales to my envious brothers, my admiring sisters, and my horrified mother. But I was still worried and couldn't rid myself of the terrible sense of being watched. Perhaps the Bangallans were, at that very second, floating somewhere above the ship, as invisible as the air we breathed. There were other things that worried me, too. Several of the crew members had decided to remain on the island, and my father's attempts to change their minds, or to enlist natives to replace them, had failed. The natives were convinced that our journey was doomed, that we would not survive the passage. And so we sailed shorthanded.

As the strange ship closed in on us, it grew in both size and menace. I gazed through a spyglass my father had given me before leaving home. I found the mast and followed it upward to the top, where a flag rippled and shimmered like a mirage. I steadied my hand, squinted, then saw what looked like the shape of a spider web on the flag. My young friend had told me that the spider web was flown on the ships of the meanest and deadliest of the pirates, the ones who never spared the crew.

"Quick, Kit, get below deck!" my father shouted. "Into the cargo hold. Hide yourself among the woolens."

"I want to be up here. *Please.*"

But such fury seized my father's face that I scampered below like a terrified rat. I opened a hole in one of the bundles where I could hide. But before crawling inside, I had to find out what was happening on deck.

I crept slowly up the ladder, then nudged the hatch upward a couple of inches. I heard pounding feet trampling the deck, the firing of muskets, shouts, and horrid cries. I smelled gunpowder and saw one of the crew collapse to the deck, blood pouring from his chest.

My heart pounded as I lowered the hatch again. The Bangallan pirates had easily caught the ship. Our meager supply of firearms and skeleton crew were no match for the seasoned pirates. It seemed there was nothing I could do. But I didn't want to be a kid anymore. I wanted to help. I desperately needed to help.

I pushed against the hatch, but suddenly it was flung open. A scar-faced pirate stood above me, swinging a notched saber. Just as he slashed downward, a musket fired and the pirate toppled over. His sword fell harmlessly into the hold.

"I told you to hide!" my father shouted.

I wanted to weep in shame, to curl up into a small, tight ball and roll away. But just then, another pirate rushed forward, his face and clothing splattered with blood.

"Look out!" I screamed.

My father spun, but it was too late. A glint of sunlight from the pirate's bloodied saber flashed in my eyes, and then my father, the captain, fell to the deck, cut down by the blade.

"No! No!" I yelled, and started to scramble through the hatch. But it slammed down on my head and I tumbled into the hold and landed on a bundle of woolen goods. I started to climb the ladder again to avenge my father's death, but halfway up, I heard his voice so clearly it was as if he were standing next to me.

"Kit, follow my orders. Do it now!"

I froze, one foot halfway between two rungs, and looked around the dark cargo hold, but could see no one. Was it my imagination?

"Hurry, Kit!" the voice said.

I scrambled down the ladder and crawled into my hiding place. And there I waited, terrified, trembling. The wet smell of the wool seeped into my nostrils; the darkness crowded around me like a gang of thieves.

For the longest time, I heard screams, shouts, boots pounding the deck of the ship. Then, for an even longer time, there was a thick, horrifying stillness—the silence of the grave. I didn't move, barely breathed. The stink of the damp wool nearly choked me. My arms itched, my throat closed up, every muscle in my body shrieked for movement, flight, freedom, fresh air. I blacked out—seconds, minutes, it was impossible to tell—and when I came to, I was no longer alone in the hold.

TWO

The pirates pawed through the bales of woolen goods in the hold, their angry voices muted by the wool packed tightly around me. Even if I could have heard their words, I wouldn't have understood them. But I knew they were arguing, and it was probably about what they should do with the bales.

I considered crawling out, showing myself, surrendering. It probably meant certain death, but what difference did it make? I'd failed my father; he had died because of me, because I had failed to obey him. I deserved to die, too. The only thing I hoped was that my death would be quick and painless.

But something kept me from giving up. It was like a silent command from an invisible presence. *Dad? Are you here?* I mouthed the words silently. I wanted some sort of confirmation of what had happened earlier.

No answer.

Dad, please say something, talk to me like before, please, please . . .

Silence.

What was the use? A wave of utter desolation crashed over me. If I stayed where I was, I would die of hunger or thirst. I started to crawl out, but as soon as I pushed my head to the edge of the bale, I saw a clear image of my father standing in front of me and his voice flowed through me, as clear and warm as liquid. "Wait, Kit! Get back inside."

I did as the voice instructed, pushing myself down deeper into the bale. But through a narrow opening, I could see three pirates, their backs to me. One of them was still talking, but now in a calmer tone of voice. I sensed that a decision had been made. After that, everything grew quiet. Relief flooded through me. I could swallow again, breathe again.

Maybe they'd decided to just forget about the bales of wool. That was fine with me. I tried to imagine what might happen next. Would they sink the ship? I doubted it. The vessel was less than a year old; it made sense that they would take it as part of their booty. Hopefully they'd sail it away to sell or trade in a foreign market.

Somehow I would survive, I knew I would. I had to. Instantly I began plotting my escape. I would sneak out of the bale during the night, find food and water, then sneak back in here. That was about the best I could expect. What I dreaded was the thought that the ship might be taken to the pirates' hideout. If that was the case, my chances of escape were not very good. Even if I got away, I probably wouldn't survive. I'd heard that Bangalla was filled with wild beasts and that if the natives didn't kill you, then the animals would. What chance did a young boy have?

As I pondered these alternatives, several men entered the cargo hold. From the grunts and groans, it sounded as if they were lifting the bales and carrying them up to the deck. I had no idea whether that was good news or bad.

Finally the bale where I was hiding rocked back and forth, then was turned on its side. Muttering and an angry flurry of words followed. I didn't have to understand their language to recognize the words as curses.

Suddenly the bale was lifted and carried slowly out of the cargo hold and up to the deck. Despite the stink of the wool, I could smell the sea air, the dizzying sweetness of it, the promise of all it held. I nearly wept with relief.

The bale was dropped and struck the deck with a hard thud that jarred me to the bone. I waited to see what would happen next, but after a few minutes curiosity overcame caution. I worked my way toward the outside of the bale until I saw light. I blinked as my eyes adjusted to the sudden brightness, then saw a crooked line of bales. Two men were moving down the line tossing one bale after another from the merchant ship onto the pirates' vessel. It looked like I was going to be taking another voyage.

The men were getting closer, so I ducked back inside the bale. I curled up in a ball and waited. Moments later, the bale was rocked from side to side and I heard the same curses again. Then I was swinging in the air, back and forth, like a corpse hanging from a gallows. The bale was tossed; I was airborne.

I tensed, expecting to feel the impact against the deck at any moment. But I kept dropping, tumbling, rolling through the air. The bale missed the deck and splashed into the sea.

I bobbed on the ocean inside my cocoon, drifting with the waves. I waited for the pirates to retrieve the bale, but the minutes collapsed into each other, flattening into a thin line that seemed to go on forever. My awareness shrank until there was only the bobbing of the bale, the smell of the sea, and the waiting.

I realized then that they weren't coming after it. Maybe I was free of the pirates, but I was still lost at sea, and in serious trouble.

Most of the bale was wrapped with heavy cloth coated with a waterproof lacquer, but water was still seeping into the wool, and slowly, a bit at a time, the bale was sinking.

I worked my way toward the opening. The constant rocking and the thickness of the damp wool made it difficult to move. I was having a hard time breathing, too, as the air pockets closed around me and strands of the wool were sucked into my mouth and nose with every breath.

I started to panic and clawed madly at the wool, twisting and turning my body until I gulped at fresh air. A salty wave splashed in my face. I coughed, rubbed my hands over my face, and dropped my head back, scanning the vast, empty sky.

It was late afternoon, the wind had picked up and white caps topped the swells. I worked my way out of the bale and climbed onto it. There was no sign of the *Miranda,* my father's ship, or the pirate vessel. The day washed into evening, then night. My throat was parched, stars pulsed in the heavens, I became delirious, and I drifted. At some point, I raised my head and saw a fire burning in the distance between the star-speckled sky and the black waters. For a moment, I didn't understand how a fire could be burning on the water. Then I remembered what the boy on the island had said. The spider-web pirates always killed the crew and destroyed the ships, and I knew it was the *Miranda* burning.

My heart seized up on me then, and I began to cry, to shout, to pray. Then exhaustion swallowed me.

When I opened my eyes again, the sun had risen and my thirst was so great I began to see streams and rivers and lakes, fresh water molded and shaped by unseen hands into towns and cities that shimmered and danced in the light like living things.

In my lucid moments, I estimated that it was either midmorning or midafternoon. At some point during the night, I must have crawled between the rope holding the bale together and the wool. I couldn't recall doing it, but it was the only reason I was still alive. But I wouldn't last much longer. I needed water. I craned my head and saw palm trees and a beach. I was washing ashore. I was going to make it! But as I got closer to the beach, I was caught in the surf. A huge wave broke over me. The bale flipped over and over, and when it stopped tumbling, I was under it. I struggled wildly to free myself. I couldn't drown here, not so close to shore, so close to surviving. Then the bale rolled over again, and I gasped for air. Instantly another wave lifted me and slammed me down against the sand. Over and over, the surf pounded against the bale, spinning it around and around, battering and shredding it.

Dazed and barely able to breathe, I passed out and drifted in the backwash of my mind in a calm, pleasant place where there were no Bangallan pirates, no raging seas, a place where my father was still alive, still with me, and all was well.

*   *   *

When I woke up, I found myself caked in soggy wool and sand. I could hear the surf, but I couldn't feel it or see it. Slowly I pulled away the clumps of wool and rolled over. The surf slapped against my legs, which had grown numb with exhaustion.

I lifted my head and looked out to sea. The sun was setting. Its fiery glow on the water reminded me of the burning ship.

The memory of my father's death came back to me as I clawed my way up the beach, tiny bits of sand lodging beneath my nails like slivers of glass. Why was I still alive, while the others were dead? I wished I had gone with them. I closed my eyes and a shudder ripped through my body. I was lost, cold, and thirsty. I wouldn't last much longer.

Something caught my attention. Everything around me was quiet, but I knew I wasn't alone. My eyes fluttered open to moonlight and shadows moving over the sand. Several pairs of bare feet soon encircled me. I was afraid to raise my eyes, but I did. I followed those brown toes to their ankles, their calves, their thighs, all the way to the strange, hard faces of spear-bearing natives bent over me.

One of the natives waved a stick in front of my face. Impaled on the end of it was a human skull.

I shut my eyes, too exhausted and weak to fight or struggle. I had somehow survived the pirates and the sea only to be captured by cannibals.

THREE

I raised up on my hands and knees, but I was so weak I dropped back onto my belly. A muscular man grabbed me by the arm and jerked me into the air as though I weighed no more than a twig. Moments later I was being carried quickly and soundlessly through the jungle along an invisible trail.

Shafts of moonlight created eerie, shifting shadows that quickly revealed and concealed hints of the jungle's exotic mysteries. And these shadows were alive with animal sounds. Every time a branch scratched my back or arms, I thought a leopard was clawing me.

Sometimes the jungle was so dense there was no light at all, and I felt strange, disconnected from my body, bumping along through all the darkness like a piece of driftwood. I wondered if this was how the Bangallas felt when they left their bodies. I lost consciousness for a while and sank deeply into some other place. When I came to, we were entering a thatched village. Yes, I was terrified. But I was also filled with incredible wonder. Ever since we'd left home, I had dreamed of getting a close look at primitive jungle dwellers like those my father had seen on his voyage with Columbus. But then again, I didn't want to be the main course of their next meal, either.

I was deposited on the hard-packed ground in the center of the circle of huts. One of the men left half a coconut shell filled with water by my side. I drank deeply, my eyes darting about, watching the two men who guarded me while the rest disappeared into the huts.

Shadowy figures rippled through the moonlit night. Some stopped and stared at me; others acted as if I weren't even there. After a time, an old man appeared and crouched down a few feet away. He stared hard at me, muttered something under his breath, then signaled for the men to carry me into a hut.

The hut smelled as damp and as lush as the jungle. The old man gave me a cup of brown water that tasted like cold tea and a plate of stringy dried fish. After I ate, he motioned for me to lie down on a bedding of dried grasses. Even though my future was uncertain, I fell asleep with ease.

So began the first night of my life among the natives on the island of Touganda.

Over the following weeks, months, and years, I gradually learned the ways of the Touganda tribe. Buli, the old man who had fed me dried fish, was my teacher. He was the village spiritual leader, a powerful shaman and priest, a man of knowledge. He was a stern, demanding teacher, but he could also be kind and warmhearted.

I was surprised to learn that the Tougandas were one of the so-called savage tribes of the Bangalla jungle. But I found that, for the most part, they lived in peace with their neighbors and shared many things in common with them. One of those things was the skill of navigating the high seas and the jungle with their minds.

I remembered the boy from the island had said the Bangalla pirates used that skill to find ships to attack. Many of those pirates were not from any of the Bangallan tribes, Buli said, but they used Bangallans as navigators.

When I drew the spider-web symbol in the dirt, Buli nodded and said that the ones who had killed my father and destroyed his ship were a band of pirates who had only recently invaded these waters. They were feared by the Touganda tribe, and Buli himself was afraid that someday there would be a great battle.

I soon learned mind navigation myself. I traveled deep within the Bangalla jungle, learning its secrets, then later journeyed to other islands and other lands. Buli was an excellent teacher, but I still talked with my father's ghost. He promised me that one day very soon my life would once again take a dramatic turn.

Whenever I tried to use my newly acquired skills to locate my father's killers, I failed. Buli said the pirates' hideout was protected by powerful Bangallan sorcerers who were in league with them, men who could literally lay a blanket of invisibility over a place. But Buli promised he would use his own powers to find my father's murderers.

I was never quite sure how he intended to do this. Although his skills were formidable, I didn't think he was powerful enough to go up against sorcerers and was sure his promise would go unfulfilled.

Time passed. I never mentioned his promise and

neither did he. Then one day while I was out walking, I found a body that had washed up on the beach. I recognized the clothing as my father's, and I was certain that the man wearing the clothes was his killer.

I grabbed the collar of the shirt my father had once worn and dragged the body away from the beach to where no one but scavengers would find it. Vultures soon arrived; in a matter of days, they picked the bones clean.

I took the skull, held it up with both hands, and swore an oath. ''I will devote my life to the destruction of piracy, greed, cruelty, and injustice, and my sons and their sons shall follow me.''

I didn't tell Buli about the body or what I did with the skull. But it didn't matter. I was sure he knew exactly what I'd done. Sometimes I felt certain that he could *see* my most intimate thoughts, that they came to him as pictures, quick, brilliant flashes that told him everything he needed to know. Other times I was equally certain that I was a complete mystery to him, a puzzle of scattered, exotic pieces that he was constantly arranging and rearranging, trying to fit together.

Perhaps both were true. Perhaps we taught each other, he and I: student and teacher in interchangeable roles.

One night, he asked me to attend a ceremony. He said it would be the most important night of my life, so of course I went.

All the tribe members were assembled around a towering tree trunk when I joined them. Images of jungle spirits were carved into the trunk, etheric shapes that seemed to swirl and dance in the firelight, almost as if the images were coming to life and seeking to leap from the trunk and into the world.

They frightened me, these images. I felt they represented me and my journey from the deck of the *Miranda* to this strange jungle tribe. I, too, had sought freedom from what I was. I, too, had sought to leap full-blown into this new world.

Buli was wearing thick silver bands embedded with luminous pearls on his upper arms. In the firelight, the pearls shifted colors. One moment they were as pale and insubstantial as ghosts, and in the next moment, they burned like the sky at sunset.

He stood in front of the spirit shrine, his arms raised, his eyes rolling back in his head. Then he rubbed a vivid purple paint onto his forehead, over his cheeks and jaws. He looked like a massive bruise.

On a shelf that protruded from the shrine stood three intricately carved skulls. One skull was made of gold, another of silver, the third of jade. I knew these were the ancient, powerful Skulls of Touganda that I'd heard about but never seen. The fact that I was being allowed to see them now shocked me nearly as much as the sight of the skulls themselves.

They were incomparably beautiful—every facet and surface so perfectly carved, it was as if they had been chiseled from celestial light. The glow of the fire washed over them with the ease of a liquid, transforming them, transforming me. But in the hollows of their eye sockets lay only darkness, a black, impenetrable sea that seemed to suck at me as if to draw me in.

Drums thundered in my ears. Buli's body swayed in rhythm to their beats, as though he and the drums were one and the same. When the drums reached a crescendo, he turned in my direction and thrust a ring at me. It bore the symbol of a skull.

I raised my hand, and he slipped the ring onto my finger. It fit perfectly. As I stared at the ring, it began to glow. Rays of light shot out of it. I knew—without knowing why—that I was no longer Kit Walker, that I was now someone much different and more powerful. I squeezed my eyes shut and saw, in the shadows and tendrils of light, the new name I would take.

From this time on, I would be known as the Phantom.

FOUR HUNDRED
YEARS LATER

O

FOUR

Bangalla Jungle

After twelve years in this godforsaken jungle, Quill still hated it. He hated it more than when he had first arrived after the jailbreak in '21. And he knew he would hate it as long as he was here.

He had been trying to get out for years, and just when he thought he had found the ticket to a new life in the States, his ticket turned out to have the Bangalla jungle written all over it. So after a couple of months in New York, here he was again.

But this time he knew that if he succeeded in following his new bosses' orders, he would never set foot in this sweltering green hell again. He would be home free, and this nightmare place would be a dimming, ugly memory, nothing more. At the moment, though, the possibility seemed about as distant from him as the moon.

He slammed on the brakes of the battered, rusted cargo truck he was driving. It squealed to a stop and the engine growled, backfired, then stalled. Ahead of him, two ruts wound through the dense foliage. Hardly a road, he thought. It wasn't even a path.

He flattened the crumpled map against the steering wheel and studied it. It didn't tell him a bloody thing. How far had they come, anyway? But more importantly, how far did they still have to drive through this steaming hell?

As far as Quill was concerned, the Bangalla jungle was about the worst place in the world. You just couldn't venture into this jungle without something happening, and usually that something was bad, very bad. Sometimes he even thought that jail was better than life in the Bangalla jungle.

He'd been serving a life term for a murder he hadn't even done. Sure, he'd wasted a few guys as part of his job with the Zephro gang in New York, but he didn't kill that cop. They'd lied and cheated to put him behind bars, but he'd shown them. He'd gotten away in a big jailbreak after just two years, and they'd never caught him.

"I hate this worthless map."

"Hey, Quill. Look where you stopped. We're sinking right into the muckety-muck."

Quill glanced over at Morgan, who'd been in the jungle three years but looked like he'd been in it all of his life. With Morgan around, he didn't need a mirror. Morgan reflected Quill's own state of disrepair. They were both unshaven and sweaty, and their khaki pants and white shirts were filthy. Quill had chewed his unlit cigar to a pulp at the end; Morgan's Panama hat was smeared with mud and was so tattered, a high wind threatened to dissolve it to dust.

The only thing each man kept immaculate was his pistol. Each pistol was oiled and kept so clean even a drill sergeant would fail to find fault with it.

"So, get out and push us before we sink down to

the axle," Quill barked. "Styles and Breen, wake up!" He shook his head, muttered a curse under his breath, then shoved the native kid who was sitting between him and Morgan. "What are you looking at, you little heathen? Out! Get out! You help, too. Pushy-push. Heave-ho."

Two men, one tall and lanky with a goatee, the other short and stocky with a flattened nose, climbed from the back of the truck and joined Morgan and the kid in the mud. The tall one, Styles, promptly slipped and fell, cursing as Quill turned over the engine. The truck growled to life, backfired, stalled again.

The jungle erupted in squawks and squeals. A monkey dropped onto the hood, shook his arms, bared his teeth, and screeched. Quill pulled out his pistol and took aim, but the monkey leaped into the jungle before he fired. A moment later, a huge green seed pod was lobbed from where the monkey had disappeared. It banged hard against the windshield; a weblike crack spread soundlessly across the glass.

"Monkeys. I hate monkeys," Quill muttered, then cranked the ignition. The engine popped and growled to life. He stepped on the gas and ground the gears. The truck rocked forward and back, then forward again. The tires spun, splattering mud over the three men and the kid. Then, slowly, the rusted hulk found a footing and lumbered ahead.

Morgan and the kid raced after the truck, leaped onto the sideboard, and crawled back inside as Breen and Styles dove into the cargo area.

"You drive," Morgan said, "I'll navigate." Then he leaned over, reaching for the map, but Quill swatted his hand away.

"Problem is, the map's all wrong."

Morgan made a futile effort to wipe the mud from his pants and shirt. "Naw, the map is good. Remember its source. That man is never wrong. You said it yourself. He's the best there is."

Maybe, maybe not. That was yet to be seen.

Morgan was good at taking orders, but he didn't think things through, and that's what had probably gotten him in trouble in the past. He was another ex-con exile. At least half of the guys in Zavia, Bangalla's rough and tumble port town, were wanted for something somewhere, or they were here looking for trouble. The rest of the guys were part of the Brotherhood, a ruthless bunch who'd been around here a long time.

"Then why does it show a bridge back there?" Quill stabbed a thumb in the air over his shoulder. "We never crossed no bridge."

The kid pointed at the map and said something in the local lingo. Quill didn't understand a word of it. "What's he saying, Morgan?"

"Didn't quite catch it all. Whadya say, Zak? Say it again."

The kid turned to Morgan and repeated the same words. Morgan was married to a native woman and had picked up some of the lingo. He frowned and nodded. "Ah, let's see. Turn around. He says we better turn around."

Quill waved a hand. "Not a chance! And maybe the little quitter needs a lesson in positive thinking."

He swung the back of his hand at the kid's face. But the truck hit a hole, bounced hard, and Zak ducked out of the way. He covered his face with his arms to shield off any more blows and spoke rapidly in his Bangallan dialect.

"Wait, Quill!" Morgan yelled. "Now I get it! Turn the map around! That's what he's saying." He laughed, slapped his knee. "You got it upside down, you big moron!"

Quill glared at Morgan and Zak. This deal better work or he didn't know what he was going to do. He couldn't stand it any longer. If things didn't improve soon, he was going to lose his mind.

He rubbed the spider-web tattoo on his right forearm, as if to draw strength and patience from it. He was part of the Brotherhood, a low-level guy who'd worked his way into the outfit. Now he just wanted to use what he knew and work his way out of it.

"If the map's upside down, then there oughta be a bridge up ahead, and all I see is more jungle." He leaned forward and peered through the muddied windshield. "Oh, no!"

Quill slammed his foot down on the brake, snapping Morgan and Zak forward against the dashboard. The truck slid through the dirt and its wheels locked, brakes squealing. A huge cloud of dust billowed around the truck, engulfing it. When it finally settled, Quill saw that the truck had come to rest at the foot of a rope suspension bridge.

The two men stepped out of the truck and moved to the edge of the precipice. Quill's knees turned soft and mushy at the sight of the deep gorge that the bridge spanned. Everything spun. More than anything, he feared heights—the dizzying swirl when he peered downward; the horrifying sense that the earth was shifting beneath his feet.

He wrenched himself back from the edge, sucking

air quickly through his clenched teeth. His stomach churned. He took a long, deep breath for ballast to steady himself.

"Hey, Quill!" Breen yelled, rubbing his thick neck as he and Styles climbed out the back of the truck. "What's the deal? How about warning us when you're going to stop like that." Then he saw the bridge. "Oh, I see."

Quill took a closer look. The bridge was about thirty yards long and was constructed of thick rope and jungle vines, with a pathway made of heavy wood planks. He turned to Morgan. "Whadya think?"

"I don't know. Looks like it'll hold, but then again . . ."

"Breen? Styles?"

"Hate to bet my life on it, Quill," Breen said.

"Same here," Styles agreed.

Quill considered their situation for a few moments; his eyes were on the bridge, not the chasm. He was pretty sure he could make it across, but he didn't want to chance it with the truck.

"Okay. We'll go over on foot. All except one. He'll stay back to drive the truck across."

They all looked at one another and edged away from the bridge. "Yeah. Good idea, Quill. But which one?" Morgan asked.

Quill turned to see Zak standing in front of the truck. He smiled at the kid. "Hey, you want to learn to drive a truck?"

"You're kidding, I hope," Morgan said.

"Not unless you'd like to take his place."

When Zak slid behind the wheel, he could barely see over the dashboard. In order for his feet to reach the pedals, he had to sit on the very edge of the seat. His mouth was dry, his head ached. He was concentrating, doing what they'd told him. He knew this bridge well. He'd crossed it many times. He'd seen carts pulled by horses, but he'd never seen a truck cross over it. The bridge was old, but he thought it was strong enough to support the truck as long as he stayed on the wood planks. That was the problem. He just didn't know if he could drive it in a straight line.

He had to do it, though. He wasn't doing it for these men. No, it was for his father. These men were bad and his father needed his help. Zak would do whatever he could to free him.

The man named Quill had heard that his father knew this part of the jungle better than anyone, so one day when Zak and his father were in Zavia buying supplies, Quill asked his father to be his guide. His father agreed when he heard how much Quill was going to pay him, but he changed his mind when he found out what Quill and the other men were looking for.

That was when they took him to a ship in a cove and tied him up. They were going to torture him in front of Zak, but then Zak told the men he knew the jungle, too, and he would help them if they let his father go. Quill promised they would free his father as soon as Zak showed them the way to the ancient place.

That was the last time he had seen his father. As he'd left the ship, Zak had found his father's red and blue kerchief on the dock. He'd picked it up and still carried it with him, a reminder that his father's freedom was the only thing that mattered.

The engine was already running. He stretched forward, pushing the clutch pedal as close as he could to the floor without slipping off the seat. Then he pulled the shift stick toward him. The engine sputtered. The gears were grinding, and he wasn't sure if he was going to be able to make them work.

He followed the directions the men had given him as closely as he could. He let the clutch out slowly and stepped on the gas pedal. But the engine coughed, the truck shuddered, and then it stalled. He hadn't pushed down hard enough.

They told him that might happen. So he started over again. This time he stepped harder on the gas pedal as he let out the clutch. The truck jerked ahead, bounced onto the bridge, and Zak's breath died in his throat.

The truck rolled forward. He knew that if he drove off the planks, the bridge might sway, the ropes might break, and the truck could easily tumble over the side. He concentrated on steering, but the truck was picking up speed as it descended to the center of the bridge. He turned the wheel from side to side and somehow stayed on the planks.

Then, as the truck started ascending toward the other side, it went slower, slower. He rocked his body forward and back in the seat, as if the motion would force the truck to go faster. Almost there. Not much further. But the truck was barely moving now.

The four men on the other side urged him on, motioning wildly with their hands. "I knew that bridge was safe!" yelled the one called Styles. "He's going to make it. Step on it, kid!"

Then, from Quill: "C'mon, kid!" He grinned like

a monkey, gestured, grinned some more. "Nice and easy now. Almost there."

Quill was the meanest one of the bunch. Zak wanted to run the truck right into him. But he had to think of his father.

Then Zak's foot slipped off the gas pedal. When he tried to reach it, the wheel spun to the left, then the right. He steadied it, but the engine sputtered, then died.

"Turn it over, kid. Turn it over!" Quill yelled, no longer grinning.

Zak didn't understand. What was he saying, turn the truck over? That's what he was trying not to do.

"Start it again," Morgan shouted in his terrible attempt to speak Bangalla, the common language used by all the tribes to communicate. "Start it again."

Zak understood him the second time. He turned the key. The truck jerked forward, but didn't start.

"The clutch," one of the men yelled. "Step on the clutch!"

He pressed down with his left foot and cranked the engine again. It roared to life and he stepped down as hard as he could on the gas pedal. The truck lurched ahead onto solid ground, and the men leaped aside.

"The brake, the brake!" Quill yelled.

Zak was confused, then remembered the other pedal. He slid forward and slammed both feet onto the brake. The truck jerked to a stop. Still in gear, it sputtered, backfired, and stalled. He collapsed against the steering wheel.

The driver's door swung open, and Quill roughly pulled him out. "Look," he said, stabbing his finger in the direction of the pedals. "Brake pedal, clutch pedal. Brake pedal, clutch pedal. Got it?"

Zak felt like spitting in his face. *I'm the one who drove across it,* he thought. *I earned my father's freedom.* But he was too afraid of Quill to say anything. He didn't like the skull tattooed on his cheek or the spider web tattooed on his forearm. That, more than anything, sent bright, sharp stabs of fear through Zak.

"Ah, I'm wasting my time," Quill said with a look of disgust. He jumped in the driver's seat, put the truck in gear, and accelerated away from the bridge as the other men chased after it.

Zak just stood there and stared after the truck, relieved that he'd made it, but confused by the vision that unfolded in his mind's eye. He saw the ropes breaking, saw the truck plummeting into the ravine. Then he understood what it meant: the truck wasn't going to make it across the bridge on the return trip.

FIVE

The lush tangled forest was closing in on them with every mile they traveled. Quill imagined that if he stopped, he would actually see the vines and branches growing and slowly reaching out toward the truck. If they stayed in one place for long, the vehicle and all of its occupants would be completely strangled, victims of the cursed Bangalla jungle.

Quill slowed to a stop. The twin ruts disappeared just ahead of the truck, swallowed by a mass of green growth. A forbidding, impenetrable wall of jungle foliage blocked their way.

"End of the road, fellows," Quill said, stepping out of the truck. Their only choice was to burrow ahead. "We go on foot from here. Get the machetes out." He unfolded the map. "Zak! Take a look. Which way?"

The kid glanced at the map, then the jungle. He stepped back, shook his head, and mumbled something that was barely audible.

"What now?" Quill turned to Morgan for an explanation. "What's his problem?"

Morgan leaned over and exchanged a few words

with Zak. Straightening up, he frowned. "Says we can't go on. These woods are protected."

"Oh, yeah? By who?" Quill asked.

Morgan listened to Zak; his frown deepened to a deep furrow between his eyes. "He says ... a ghost."

Breen snorted. "A what?"

"The Ghost Who Walks," Morgan said. "That's who he's talking about."

Quill's hand tapped the skull tattoo on his face. "See that kid? Betcha don't know what it means, do you? No, of course not. You only know about superstitions. It means we don't have to worry about any Ghost Who Walks. You can be sure of that."

"Well, the little bugger says he won't take us beyond this point," Morgan said.

"Shoot him," Styles said.

"No, we may need him." Quill smiled. "To drive the truck back across the bridge. Tie him up and toss him into the back of the truck." He glanced down at the map and tapped it with his index finger. "We can find our own way from here."

It was late afternoon when Quill and his companions arrived at the face of a cliff deep in the jungle. It was right where the map had said it would be, a mile east of a pond that had taken them hours to find.

The jungle steamed, the insects were horrendous man-eaters, but the snakes were the worst. They'd killed one for every hundred yards they'd traveled. They were lucky they hadn't all been poisoned or squeezed to death by the deadly serpents.

They had been taking a break when Quill had spotted something glistening through the foliage. The pond. From there they had followed the compass readings and headed directly east. They'd climbed and crawled and scrambled through the jungle, hacking their way through the underbrush as best they could to maintain a straight path through the thicket, until finally the cliff was visible.

Now that they were there, they had to find the cave, and so far there was no sign of it.

The jungle guarded its secrets like a jealous lover, thought Quill. He slashed his machete at the underbrush, working his way along the base of the cliff. This must be the right cliff, he kept telling himself. He'd covered about twenty feet when he came to a narrow opening in a rock. Suddenly filled with new energy, he chopped vigorously at the vines growing over the opening and pulled them away with his hands.

The mouth of the cave was actually no more than a crack in the cliff. If he hadn't known there was a cave, he would never have found the opening. He still wasn't sure this was the right place. He stuck his head through the opening and yelled. His voice echoed, a strange hollow sound that bounced off walls deep inside the cliff. The cave, for sure.

"Over here!" he shouted. He didn't know if the others heard him; they were chopping along other parts of the cliff. "Hurry up. We haven't got all day."

Instead of waiting for the others, Quill squeezed through the crack. The dampness suffused his senses; he blinked hard against the darkness and waited a moment for his eyes to adjust to the light that filtered in through the opening.

He had the odd feeling that he was being observed.

He turned on his flashlight; the beam bounced off the wall across from him. Shadows eddied across it, and for a moment he thought one shadow seemed longer than the others, denser. It spooked him. He blinked and it was gone.

He listened, but didn't hear any sounds from within the cave. Too much jungle, he thought. The blasted jungle was playing tricks on his head, messing with his eyes.

As the others joined him, they turned on their flashlights. Quill had barely gone fifteen feet into the cave when he froze in place. His beam of light played on a blackened, shriveled corpse that was leaning against the wall. Its lips had long ago disappeared; it looked like a grotesque, grinning demon.

He turned and there was another and another. Everywhere they looked they saw decomposing, semi-mummified corpses propped up in niches and alcoves that had been cut in the wall.

"It's a crypt," Quill whispered.

"Uncle Leo!" Breen said, aiming his light at a withered corpse. A thick, hairy spider had woven a web between the remains of the face and the shoulders. When the light struck the web, the creature darted inside an eye socket.

"Knock it off!" snapped Morgan.

Quill didn't like it. He couldn't shake the feeling that they were being observed. Softly he said, "Keep your eyes open."

Styles didn't like this cave; not a bit. He wished he had waited outside. He could've said he'd guard the entrance. But now it was too late. If he said anything, Quill would accuse him of being afraid of the dark. He'd never let up on him.

Styles squatted down in front of the corpse and scratched his scruffy goatee. He leaned forward and scrutinized the silver armbands. Some sort of jewels were imbedded in the silver. "You look like an important fella. Let me see what you left behind."

Cautiously he reached out and rubbed one of the stones on an armband. It looked like a pearl, he thought. He was about to see if he could slip the armbands off when he noticed several baskets partially covered with rotting fabric near the corpses' feet. He opened one and saw that it was filled with precious stones. So was the next one and the one after that. He could hardly contain himself. He'd struck it rich.

He was about to call the others over when he saw something wrapped in a cloth behind the baskets. He leaned forward and scooped up the oval object. The cloth nearly disintegrated in his hands, and he was left holding a soiled and discolored skull.

But from the weight of it, he knew it was no ordinary skull. He buffed the crown with the sleeve of his shirt and a silvery sheen glimmered in the flashlight's beam. "Hey, Quill! Over here!"

"Whadya find?"

He held up the skull and grinned, and the jeweled eyes glowed as if with a light of their own. "I think you're going to like this. I got it."

"Good work, Styles!" He cupped the skull in his palms and studied it. "Well, well. Mr. Drax is gonna be very happy."

Styles was wondering about his bonus, and what they were going to do with all the jewels and old stuff that looked like it was made of gold and silver. If he became rich, the first thing he intended to do was to get out of this jungle and go back to the States. But he needed some cover or the cops would be all over him. They'd been after him for years.

"Hey, Quill, I was just wondering, what's so important about that thing, anyway?"

Quill was silent a moment. "I dunno. I don't like to ask Drax too many questions." He lowered the skull. "His answers scare me."

"So how did you get connected with him? I'm thinking that maybe I could go to work for him, too."

"Yeah, maybe. You know I used to be with the Zephro gang back in the old days, and when I snuck back to see about getting on with them again, the boss told me to go see Drax. Said he was the one to get hooked up with now."

"So what did you tell Drax that made him hire you?" Styles asked, his curiosity growing.

"A bunch of stuff, but when I told him about the Brotherhood, he got real interested and put me to work. I thought he liked the reference, but the next thing I know he sends me right back here with that map."

"I've got another surprise for you." He smiled broadly as he opened the top of one of the baskets and Quill directed a beam of light into it.

Quill made an animal sound. "All right! Styles, why didn't ya say something? Are all the baskets—"

"Yup. You got it. They're all stuffed with jewels. We're rich, Quill. Really rich. So maybe you can put a word in for me with Drax, see, because I need the protection.''

''Yeah, I think I could . . .''

What the . . . ! A pair of cold hands clasped Styles by the neck and squeezed hard. At first he thought it was Breen or Morgan trying to scare him. But when he reached up to pull off the hands, he grabbed bony arms and bony fingers. He jerked wildly at the arms, gagging, gasping for air. But the corpse had him.

Quill took a step back, stunned by the animated corpse. He hesitated, then dropped the skull and tried to pry off the fingers, but they tightened around Styles's neck. He pulled out his gun and fired several times into the corpse. It didn't do any good.

Styles's struggling was futile. His life was slipping away, and his past unreeled in the shadows dancing on the cave walls. He saw himself as an altar boy in Philadelphia, getting caught stealing candy from a store, breaking into houses as a teenager, going to war, coming home, and killing a bank teller and two cops in a robbery. He'd been on the run when he'd met Morgan and Breen, who were also in big trouble. Then Quill came along and promised them all a good life in a faraway paradise working for the Sengh Brotherhood, whoever they were.

Some paradise. Apes and insects, snakes and crocodiles, even lions. The jungle was more dangerous than death row. And he still didn't know anything about the Sengh Brotherhood, except that the jungle held their deadly secrets. That thought hung in front of him like a solid thing, then it faded and Styles didn't think anymore about anything.

*   *   *

Morgan and Breen rushed over at the sound of gunfire, but there was nothing they could do. The corpse released Styles and he slumped forward.

"He's dead," Quill said flatly, and scooped up the silver skull. He turned it over and over again in his hands, and rubbed his fingers over it, checking it for nicks, chips, damage. But it seemed to be okay.

He clutched it to his chest and backed away from the grotesque corpse.

"What happened?" Morgan hissed.

"The corpse came alive! Choked him to death." Quill kept an eye on the corpse as he spoke.

"That's not possible," Morgan replied, his voice betraying the uncertainty he felt—the fear.

"Tell Styles."

"C'mon," Morgan said softly, his voice quavering now. "Let's get out of here and fast."

"Look at the jewels!" Breen said. One of the baskets had fallen over and jewels had spilled out onto the floor of the cave. "There's a lot of valuable junk in here."

Quill just wanted to get out. He wasn't taking any chances. He stuffed the silver skull into his leather pouch. "Take it. Go ahead. Take it all! Nobody's gonna miss it."

Morgan's greed overcame his fear. He tugged on his battered Panama hat and joined Breen in looting the crypt, filling burlap sacks with booty.

Quill moved toward the entrance of the cave. He was so concerned with avoiding the corpses that he walked into a spider web. He swatted at it, peeling the sticky stuff away from his face. His heart pounded in tandem with the sound of distant drumming that was seeping into the cave.

Morgan's head snapped up. "What's that noise?"

"Drums," Breen said.

"I know that. But . . . what's it mean?"

"Nuthin'," Quill hissed. "Doesn't mean nuthin'." He looked over at Styles lying facedown and the corpse resting in its niche, its empty black eye sockets staring ahead. "But hurry up, c'mon, let's get outta here."

SIX

The pounding of the drums grew in intensity and echoed through the rain forest. The thunderous beat reached into a hidden cavern decorated with a distinctive skull motif. The drum's message alerted its sole inhabitant, beckoning him from his hidden lair. But the man remained seated on his throne. His eyes were closed as if he were asleep, but he was awake and aware.

He was seeing, hearing, feeling the jungle's reactions to the drums. Flocks of birds took flight as the beat intensified. Monkeys screeched and swung in packs from tree to tree. A lion lifted its head to listen. Crocodiles basking on the banks of a river, skidded into the water and drifted through the sunlight. The wind howled through the trees and seemed to cry out, *Phan-tom, Phantom* . . . He heard and saw all of it and more.

He followed the message inscribed in the beat of the drums and listened to the guidance of forest spirits. Intruders were pillaging a sacred burial place. In his mind's eye, he saw the cliff and the secret entrance to the cave. He knew exactly where it was. He felt a sense of urgency and blinked open his eyes.

He stepped away from the Skull Throne and slipped from the shadowy depths of the cavern. His sharp eyes were masked. Like another layer of skin, a purple bodysuit fit his powerful form, rising up over his head in a tight hood. At his waist was a double-holster gunbelt with a skull insignia on the front, and on his feet were black riding boots. The skull ring on his right hand completed the distinctive ensemble.

"Devil, our help is needed again," the Phantom's deep voice resonated.

A gray Bangallan mountain wolf rose to its feet and lumbered after its master into the forest. There the Phantom whistled softly and a white stallion pranced over to him. He leaped onto its back, slipping his feet into the silver stirrups. A gentle tap at the stallion's sides sent the horse galloping down the trail, the wolf loping gracefully in his wake.

The Phantom rode with the wind at his back and breathed in the warm, humid air. It smelled rich, familiar, with all the odors he associated with home. He enjoyed riding Hero, enjoyed the freedom of the outdoors, but at the same time he steeled himself for the confrontation with the grave robbers.

He had no idea who they were, but he would find out soon enough. He urged his mount on, and they dashed through Whispering Grove en route to the sacred crypt.

The Phantom arrived at his destination just in time. He watched from a sheltered place as three grizzled men emerged from the cave. One held a black leather satchel close to his chest. The other two carried cloth sacks that looked as if they were heavy with loot from the cave.

The sight of intruders desecrating any burial site usually enraged the Phantom to action. But this place was special to him, literally a part of his heritage. Among the ancestors resting within the crypt was Buli, the great shaman-priest of the Touganda, who long ago had initiated an outsider into the tribe's ancient lineage of power.

"I never thought I'd be glad to see this jungle again, but that place gives me the creeps," said a man wearing a battered Panama hat.

"At least that crazed drumming has stopped," said one with a skull tattoo on his cheek. He took out a cigar and bit off the end of it. "I never cared much for restless natives."

At that moment, the Phantom urged Hero forward and the white horse thrashed through the underbrush, hoofs thundering against the turf. Just as the men turned to see what the commotion was about, the majestic stallion reared up on its hind legs and pawed the air several feet over their head. They threw up their arms and scrambled back, panicked and confused.

"What the heck is that?" Panama Hat yelled, staring up at the purple being.

"Shoot him!" shouted Skull Tattoo as the cigar fell from his mouth.

The short stocky man pulled a machine gun from the sack and fired wildly. The Phantom ducked, and with blinding speed drew both of his pistols and fired back. The machine gun flew from the man's hands.

"Oh, no!" shouted Panama Hat.

"Run!" Skull Tattoo yelled.

The three men darted into the jungle. Hero bolted after them, but the underbrush slowed the horse and gave the men an edge. But not for long. The Phantom found a narrow trail and sent the stallion charging down it toward the man who had fired the machine gun. The gap quickly closed. The man looked back at the horse and dropped his sack of booty to lighten his load. But he was still no match for Hero.

Without breaking stride, the Phantom reached down, grabbed the man by the back of the collar and jerked him a foot off the ground. The man's short legs pumped uselessly in the air as the Phantom carried him forward and he screamed in terror.

"Ahhhhhh!"

Then he saw what the Phantom had in mind as a huge tree trunk loomed ahead. "Noooo!"

The Phantom slammed the man's head into the trunk so hard he would be seeing stars for years to come. He dropped the looter and turned to the wolf. "Watch him, Devil. If he moves, eat him."

Devil remained behind as the Phantom galloped onward in pursuit of the other two.

Quill and Morgan, gasping for breath, burst out of a tangle of jungle and onto the road where the truck was parked. They clambered into the cab; Quill cranked the engine and slapped the accelerator to the floor. The engine promptly flooded. "C'mon, start, you sonuva . . ." The engine popped and rumbled to a start.

Morgan's head snapped this way and that, looking for the weirdo on the horse. "What about Breen, man? We can't leave him back there."

"Tough luck. Forget 'im."

"What kind of Bangallaman was that back there?" Quill ignored him. He knew exactly what they had just run into, but he didn't want to think about it right now. It just didn't make sense. No way could he accept what he'd seen. He'd already killed Ghost Who Walks. The Phantom was dead.

The truck groaned as he spun the steering wheel and swung into a U-turn. Finally they roared away and Quill patted the leather pouch, feeling the skull inside. It wasn't exactly a perfect operation, but it was a successful one as far as he was concerned. Mr. Drax would be very pleased. Maybe he'd even get a second skull tattoo to match the one he already had.

The Phantom knew the jungle—its darkest places, its secrets, its rivers, and the spots where roads intersected. He took the shortest route to the road in order to head off the grave robbers before they reached the rope bridge.

He rode hard, but Hero was tireless. When he finally emerged on the road, he spurred his mount and galloped ahead, knowing he had outdistanced the truck.

As he passed underneath a tree, the Phantom stood up in his stirrups and grabbed the lowest branch. He flipped himself over it with the agility of a gymnast and disappeared into the tree's foliage. Hero raced on down the road.

Quill gripped the wheel tightly, shifted gears, and stomped on the gas pedal. The truck bounced hard on its bad springs. He'd forgotten all about the rope bridge, but he'd deal with that when the time came. For now he was content to put as much distance as he could between himself and that purple nightmare.

Morgan was finally catching his breath. He wiped his face and neck with his bandanna, then tossed the sack of gemstones through the opening behind him, into the cargo area. It landed next to Zak, the young native guide, who was still bound and gagged.

"You know something about that guy back there, don't you, Quill? What's going on? Who is he?"

Quill took out a new cigar and stuck it in his mouth. "He's somebody I already killed."

"What?"

"It was years go, before your time. I'll tell you about it sometime."

"He didn't look very dead to me." Morgan glanced back uneasily, making sure the purple rider wasn't gaining on them.

Quill mulled over his last encounter with the Phantom. He'd bled like anyone else, and he'd died. No doubt about it.

"You may have thought you killed him," Morgan said, interrupting the silence, "but you must've only wounded him, Quill."

"I killed him. Period."

"Well, guess what—he's back!"

"He's behind us, don't worry about it."

The Phantom crouched low on the branch as the truck approached and waited until the last moment. He timed his leap perfectly and landed on the truck's hood with a loud thump. He looked straight through the cracked windshield at the two men.

"Hey, Quill!" Panama Hat shouted. "He's right in front of us!"

The cigar dropped from Quill's mouth. "Holy . . . Shoot him, Morgan! Hurry! Shoot him!"

Morgan pulled out his gun and fired. The windshield shattered and the Phantom tumbled off the right side of the hood.

Morgan knocked the jagged slivers of glass from the windshield with the handle of his gun. ''Did I get him? You see him anywhere?''

''I don't see him. You musta hit him. Unless he fell off. He's done for, anyhow.''

''Maybe we should go back and be sure. We'll finish him off if he's still breathing.''

Quill thought about it, but not for long. ''Forget it. Let's just get out of here.''

The Phantom squatted on the passenger-side fender. Then, staying low, he sidled onto the running board. Suddenly, he sprang up and slammed his fist through the glass, striking Morgan in the side of the face and knocking him senseless.

In a single swift, fluid motion, the Phantom opened the door, grabbed Morgan's limp body, and hurled him into the jungle. Then he took Morgan's place in the passenger seat.

''Sorry about the window,'' the Phantom said. ''It couldn't be helped.'' He jerked his thumb toward the smashed side window.

Surprised but unfazed, Quill swung his shoulder pouch at the Phantom. It struck him against the face. Whatever was inside was hard and heavy. The Phantom shook off the blow and grabbed the satchel by its strap. He jerked on it; Quill jerked back. A brief tug-of-war ensued, and that was when the Phantom spotted a spider-web tattoo on Quill's forearm.

Quill twisted and pulled on the pouch, trying to steer the truck at the same time. As he did so, the silver skull rolled out and across the seat.

The Phantom, already stunned by the sight of the tattoo, was briefly distracted by the skull. In the instant that the Phantom lost his concentration, Quill's hand slipped into the pouch. He pulled a knife and slashed at the Phantom, stabbing him in the side.

The pain was sharp, bright, excruciating. The Phantom grabbed the wound and Quill slammed his elbow into the Phantom's jaw. He was flung backward through the open passenger door and nearly tumbled out. Just in time, he grabbed the door frame, pulling himself part way back into the truck.

"See ya, pal," Quill said. "Keep the truck. It's all yours." With that, he scooped up the skull and bailed out the door.

The Phantom glanced up; the truck careened onto the rope bridge, out of control. It would never make it across the bridge. But if he leaped out, he'd plummet into the deep gorge to the rocks below, to an instant death.

SEVEN

The front wheels of the truck slipped off the wood planks and the Phantom was pitched out of the cab. But he grabbed the open door again and clung to it as the truck shuddered, stalled, and stopped in the middle of the bridge.

The bridge's ropes creaked as it swung above a deep gorge. An endless gorge. If he believed the native lore, then nothing could hurt him, even a plunge from this bridge. But the Phantom knew better. Carefully he shifted his weight and the door swung inward.

He pulled himself back inside the truck. But the shift of his weight caused it to rock, and the bridge swayed like a tree in high winds. The Phantom looked down only once, but it was enough. His head spun; he nearly puked. The stab wound in his side ached and throbbed. He was losing an alarming amount of blood, and he couldn't think straight enough to figure out what to do.

He knew this bridge well, and he knew that it wasn't strong enough to hold a truck for long. But how much time did he have? Seconds? Minutes?

He looked through the canvas opening in the back

of the cab and was shocked to see a native kid, bound and gagged on the floor of the cargo area. The Phantom struggled toward the opening, climbed through it, and moved over to the kid.

His side shrieked as he untied the boy. The truck kept rocking, the bridge swaying, his stomach rolling. They moved to get out. The bridge wouldn't last much longer. Already a part of him could feel its ropes fraying, giving way to the weight.

"Ghost Who Walks!" the kid gasped as the Phantom pulled out the gag. His eyes had widened with amazement, and he literally looked as if he'd seen a ghost. "You saved me."

"Not yet, I haven't. Who are you?"

"Zak." He pointed to the Phantom's wound and spoke rapidly in Bangalla.

"Sticker bush," the Phantom said, dismissing the injury, yet sucking in his breath at a stab of pain.

A sharp crack echoed through the air; it sounded like a tree splitting in half and jerked the Phantom to full awareness. The truck jerked to one side.

"The bridge is breaking," Zak whispered as though the softness of his voice might somehow prevent this from happening. "We need to get out of here."

"I know." The Phantom's voice sounded more casual than he felt. A gnawing anxiety ripped through him. "We really should be leaving."

The truck jerked again, followed by an outbreak of popping and snapping as ropes and vines broke apart, like the crackling of a thousand fires. It tilted to the right, balancing on the edge of the bridge. The Phantom and Zak slid feet-first to the wall. The bridge was now a huge rope swing, swaying under the weight of the truck, moaning like a creature in pain. Then it twisted and the truck flipped over as the Phantom and Zak tumbled onto the canvas roof.

The truck now seemed to hover above the abyss like a wad of spit in the wind. It was held in place by nothing more than a tangle of ropes and vines.

The Phantom quickly assessed the gravity of their situation, and it was about as bad as bad could get. The canvas roof was the only thing between them and the abyss. If they didn't escape, it meant the kid would never see sixteen, and the Phantom's own death would spell the end of a four hundred-year reign.

Then the truck stopped moving. The moaning ceased. Air escaped through the kid's clenched teeth. "I think it's okay now," the Phantom said.

As soon as he spoke, the rotting canvas started to rip apart. The tear spread quickly, unzipping their floor, leaving a gaping hole. Zak started slipping and shrieked, *"Help me, I'm falling!"*

His legs vanished through the opening, then his chest and head disappeared. The Phantom lunged for him, grabbed his hand. But the hole ripped wider, and the Phantom tumbled through the roof after him.

As the abyss rushed toward him and the wind whistled in his ears, the Phantom's arm shot out and hooked a vine that hung several feet below the bridge. He carefully pulled Zak up onto his back. As they dangled underneath the truck and above the gorge, the Phantom reached up with his free hand and grabbed the vine. The truck shifted. The bridge squeaked and groaned.

More ropes snapped, and one whipped the Phantom's leg. Wood planks flipped through the air, just missing their heads. The Phantom gripped the vine more tightly and tried to calm Zak, who was clinging tightly to him. "Don't be afraid."

Zak squeezed his eyes shut. "I'm not afraid with you here."

You should be, the Phantom thought. He felt blood oozing down his side, over his hip, down his leg. *Fast,* he thought. The bridge jerked twice under the weight of the truck. The remaining ropes were starting to unravel.

The Phantom saw one chance. The vine on which they were hanging was connected on one side to the wall of the gorge and on the other to the bridge. He pulled out his gun and fired. The bullet snapped the vine's connection to the bridge, and they swung free just as the bridge broke apart. The tangle of ropes and truck and vines plunged down scarcely a second after they sailed out of its path and landed on a narrow spit of rock that was barely wide enough to stand on.

The Phantom looked down as he heard the truck smash against a dry riverbed far below.

"Ungabo!" Zak exclaimed.

"You can say that again!"

The Phantom caught his breath, pressed a hand to his injured side. Hanging from the bridge had opened the knife wound even more. He had lost more blood than he cared to think about. His head started to spin again, black stars exploding in the corners of his eyes. He knew he was about to pass out. He dropped to his knees and leaned against the wall.

"What's wrong, Ghost Who Walks?" Zak gave him a quizzical look as if he didn't understand that the Phantom could feel pain or sustain an injury.

"I'm just a little tired, kid. As soon as I get my second wind, I'll be all right."

He wanted to close his eyes and sleep for a while, but he knew that would be a big mistake. He might never wake up. With an effort, he pulled himself to his feet. He raised his head and looked at the steep cliff rising in front of him. It was nearly vertical, a smooth wall of rock that extended at least a hundred feet to the rim. They were clear of the bridge, but they weren't out of the abyss. Not yet.

He felt woozy and tried to focus his mind and reach into the depths of his stamina. But his knees buckled and he collapsed against the wall again.

"Ghost Who Walks, why don't you fly out of here like they say you can do?"

"I don't fly, Zak," the Phantom said as he focused his wavering vision on the vine they had swung on, which hung down from the rim. In ordinary circumstances, climbing up the vine would be a snap, even with Zak on his back. But right now he wouldn't make it up more than a few feet off the ledge.

He needed an energy boost, something that would give him the power and strength to scale the wall. There was only one thing he knew of that could provide such a jolt of power. Still on his knees, he took the skull ring on the finger of his right hand and turned the skull inward to the palm side of his hand.

The skull ring was only to be used in dire circumstances—when death was the only alternative. He took a deep breath, then exhaled as he pressed the skull to his solar plexus, closing his eyes and concentrating. Warmth suffused his body. He felt as if he were glowing.

He pulled the ring away from his chest and blinked

his eyes open. The pain in his side had receded. He felt as if he'd just slept ten hours. He stood up and turned to Zak, who was watching him closely.

"Are you okay?" Zak asked.

"We'll see soon enough. The Phantom grabbed the vine and tested its strength. "Okay, climb on my back. We're going up."

The Phantom looked up and imagined himself moving smoothly and easily up the wall. Then he did just that, pulling himself and Zak arm over arm along the vine, striding like a fly along the smooth wall.

"That was easy," he said when they reached the top. Then the pain returned, and his legs began to wobble. Quickly he whistled, and a few moments later, Hero pranced out of the forest. After the surge of strength on the wall, the Phantom was barely able to mount Hero. He lifted Zak up to sit behind him, wincing at the resulting bite of pain.

"Take me home, Hero."

Corporal Samuel Weeks pulled into the Bangalla Jungle Patrol Headquarters and slammed on the brakes. He bounded out of his patrol truck as several patrolmen hustled two prisoners from the rear compartment.

One of the prisoners, a smart-mouthed fellow named Morgan, cursed as he was led to the main building. The other one, Breen, was injured and being held up by two patrolmen. Both were *bonos,* a local term for the foreigners who hung around Zavia. Over the years, the *bonos* had turned the fishing village into a denizen of depravity, and Weeks was grateful he didn't have to patrol the place.

Patrolling the jungle was another matter altogether. Just when you thought nothing interesting was ever going to happen, something unexpected turned up. That was the case today. A tribesman had stopped their patrol vehicle and relayed a message from deep in the jungle that looters had been seen breaking into an old burial site.

They had no trouble finding the one named Morgan. He was battered and crazed when they had arrested him and babbling about a purple giant. Some of the men thought he had jungle fever, but Weeks took his comments seriously. He asked Morgan to describe the so-called giant. All the details fit what Weeks knew, but he didn't bother to tell Morgan.

The official policy was to ignore all reports about anything related to the Phantom, the legendary Ghost Who Walks. The theory, Weeks supposed, was that if you ignored something long enough, it eventually would disappear. But it was a theory to which Weeks didn't subscribe.

Morgan had led them to his buddy, Breen, and they'd recovered two sacks of jewels and gold artifacts, which Weeks now slung over his shoulder. Their arrival set off a flurry of activity in the usually sedate outpost at the jungle's edge. Weeks dropped the sacks and saluted his commander, Captain Philip Horton, who had just stepped out of the main building to see what was going on.

"What do you have here, Corporal—poachers?" Horton's disdain was evident in his voice, in his sour expression. He was a broad-shouldered man with a thick mustache and dark bulging eyes. Weeks was thin and wiry.

"Looters, Captain. They broke into an ancient

burial cave and stole some jewels." He opened one of the bags for the captain. "Really upset some of the natives. They revere their ancestors, you know."

"So I've heard."

Weeks turned to the patrolmen. "Put them in the guardhouse."

Morgan struggled and two other patrolmen rushed forward to subdue him. "You got a problem, Captain!" Morgan yelled. "You got a 'thing' out there, a big, strange-looking purple thing! On a horse . . . with a wolf!"

Horton motioned for Morgan to be taken away. "Get him out of here."

Horton turned on his heels and walked toward a drab wooden one-story building. Weeks picked up the sacks and fell into step beside him. "That man's been chewing on the wrong kind of jungle growth," Horton said. "He's out of his mind."

"You know what he's talking about, Captain. We both do."

"Not now, Weeks. I'm not in the mood." He took the sacks of jewels from the corporal. "I'll see that these artifacts are returned to tribal authorities," he said and walked on.

"The Ghost Who Walks," Weeks called after him. "The Phantom."

"It's nonsense!"

"When you're in the jungle long enough, *anything* is possible," Weeks muttered.

In the two years that Weeks had spent patrolling the tribal territories, rarely a month went by without word of a sighting of the notorious purple marauder. Weeks figured that the Phantom was real enough, all right, but he wasn't sure how much of the legend was true. As far as he was concerned, no one lived four hundred years.

He didn't know if people could fly around outside their bodies or do all the strange things the tribal people said the Phantom could do. A lot of that was folklore, but he'd heard other things that people had actually seen.

One night when they were sharing a bottle of Bangalla blue brandy Horton had told Weeks that the Phantom had once taken out half a regiment of goons from the Sengh Brotherhood by himself. He went on to say that even though the Sengh Brotherhood was the most vicious and greedy outfit around, they had repeatedly failed to eliminate their nemesis. Since the patrol had very little success in countering the Brotherhood, Horton was pleased with the Phantom's deeds, and that he was still around. Or so he'd said on that one occasion when he'd admitted the man existed.

But it was still a confusing matter, because he'd also heard from more than one source that the secretive Sengh Brotherhood had killed the Phantom a decade ago. Then a couple of years later, reports of sightings of the Phantom started up again. At first, they were disregarded. But over time, more and more people saw the purple specter. Horton might now call it nonsense, but as far as Weeks was concerned, the Phantom was alive and well and an asset to Weeks's own work.

Horton reached the steps leading to the porch of his office. He paused, one foot on the first step, turned, and stroked his thick mustache.

"Look up the word 'phantom' in the dictionary. It means something that isn't there. Just like this ghost of yours. . . . He isn't there. He's something people see when they've got nothing better to talk about. Got it, Corporal?''

Weeks straightened his back. ''Yes, sir. Anything you say, sir.''

Horton sighed deeply, shook his head, and continued up the steps.

''Captain! Captain!''

Weeks turned and saw that another patrol vehicle had just pulled in, and Sergeant Cummings was lumbering toward them, huffing, his fat jiggling. He was at least thirty pounds overweight and reminded Weeks of a bulging sack of flour with legs. He ran past Weeks and stopped at the bottom of the steps. ''The bridge . . . sir . . . the bridge . . .''

Horton placed his hands on his hips. ''What is it, Cummings? Speak up.''

''The old rope bridge. . . . It's out.''

''Well, that was bound to happen. It's at least fifty years old.''

''But, sir . . . there was a truck on it.''

''What do you mean there was a truck on it?''

Cummings gasped for air. ''The truck is at the bottom of the gorge, and . . .''

''And, what?'' Horton snapped impatiently. ''Get it out, man.''

''We found a man who saw it go down. One of the *bonos* from Zavia. He said . . . he said that the Phantom was in the truck.''

Horton's back stiffened. ''What man? Who said that? Where is he?''

Cummings looked uneasy. ''Um, we gave him a ride out to the main road.''

''You what?''

"I didn't think to bring him here. I mean, he didn't do nothin' wrong or anything. I don't think." His words trailed off, and he scuffed his boot against the ground and coughed.

"I'll agree with that. You don't think." Horton pointed to the patrol truck. "Go find him. Weeks, you go with him. I want to talk to that man."

"You want us to go to Zavia to bring in a *bono?*" Weeks asked incredulously.

For years the patrol had considered the town off-limits. There was an unwritten agreement that the Brotherhood handled law enforcement in the town. The only time the patrol got involved was when an incident involved the tribal peoples.

"Find him, wherever he is," Horton ordered.

The Phantom sat upright, his back rigid. He breathed evenly, telling himself over and over that there was no pain, no pain. He felt nothing, only numbness.

"Hold still now," said Guran, a gray-haired native who was the Phantom's trusted assistant and the caretaker of Skull Cave.

"I *am* holding still." He took a deep breath, exhaled, and, following his training, sent a message to his side that he would feel no pain. He knew he could control pain. He'd done it before. But sometimes when he was with Guran, he felt as if he were a child again.

He held up his purple jerkin, which was raised above his wound. Slowly and carefully, Guran applied a jungle remedy that he'd mixed together in a wooden bowl.

The Phantom didn't like the look of the yellow

paste, so he turned his attention back to the book that was open on the desk in front of him. He was in the Chronicle Chamber, deep inside Skull Cave. The walls were lined with oversized leather-bound journals documenting the Phantom legacy, as well as books that had been collected from all over the world. Many were centuries old.

"Ow! Don't press so hard."

Guran rolled his eyes. "Did that sting a little?"

The Phantom shot him an irritated look, then turned his attention back to the book, pushing aside the pain. He carefully turned a yellowed page of parchment. The quill-pen handwriting was florid in style and difficult to read. But a sketch of three skulls caught his attention.

"Ah, here it is. This is what I'm looking for. The Skulls of Touganda!"

Guran glanced at the page and nodded.

"One is made of gold, another of silver, a third of jade," the Phantom explained.

"Are they valuable?"

"More than that, Guran . . . they're dangerous. When placed together, it's said the three skulls harness an energy a thousand times greater than any force or high explosive known to man."

Guran didn't react.

"It's all right here in the chronicles," the Phantom continued. "A long time ago, the Touganda tribe possessed the skulls and knew the secret of keeping their force contained."

"What happened to them? I don't know that tribe," Guran asked as he stirred the yellow paste.

"Their village was attacked by pirates of the Sengh Brotherhood. The tribe was destroyed, but three of their shamans hid the skulls in separate places before the final deadly assault. The shamans were all killed and the skulls were never found. That was four centuries ago, and there's been no trace of them . . . until today.''

Satisfied, the Phantom closed the book. Guran shrugged and started to apply his poultice again.

''That's enough, Guran. I'm quite fine, really. Good as new.''

He was ready to return to his private chamber to rest and recover. There he would finally take off his outfit and give it to Guran for cleaning and repair. While Zak was in Skull Cave, though, the Phantom would avoid stepping outside his own chamber without donning his mask and garb. Except for Guran, his identity was a well-kept secret. Although he often traveled undisguised, no one, except his assistant, knew him as both the Phantom and as Kit. As it was, Guran never called him either of those names.

''Very well, Ghost Who Walks. Maybe later. Your recovery has been impressive.'' Guran picked up his bowl and left the chamber.

The Phantom adjusted his torn jerkin and carried the journal back to the shelves. Skull Cave had a remarkable healing effect on him, and he was just glad that he'd been able to hang on to Hero until he and Zak had arrived.

As he turned to leave, he suddenly tensed. The shrouded figure of a man stood in the shadows watching him. ''Who's there?''

EIGHT

The man moved out of the shadows and into the light. He was older than the Phantom, dressed in a long robe. The Phantom's heart swelled. "Dad . . ."

"I used to come here myself, Kit, to consult the chronicles for guidance and wisdom. Usually when I was troubled, or confused." He smiled. "Or when I had just screwed up real bad."

"Guilty on all counts, Dad." A couple of beats passed. He shook his head. "I let one of the Skulls of Touganda slip right through my fingers."

"Well, don't be too hard on yourself. We all make mistakes."

The Phantom stepped closer to get a better look at his father, whom he hadn't seen in a couple of years. "This one gets worse."

"How so?"

"It was the Sengh Brotherhood."

His father frowned. "Are you sure?"

The Phantom's hands curled into fists, his shoulders tensed. He was angry at himself, and that anger wrapped around him like a sheet of cold air. "Yes, I'm sure. I saw the spider-web tattoo—the mark of the Brotherhood—right here on his arm."

His father considered the new development in silence. And somehow that silence affected the Phantom just as it had when he was a boy. Some things, he thought, never change.

When his father finally spoke, his words were uttered in a voice so soft that the Phantom could barely hear what he said. But with each word his voice grew louder, more intense, reflecting his concern and anger.

"You turned over one of the Skulls of Touganda to the Sengh Brotherhood? The most evil vermin ever to draw breath!" His father lifted his head higher, and his whole being seemed to literally rise from the floor as he continued his diatribe. "I can't believe it! They've tried and failed to get their hands on those skulls for the last four hundred years!"

The air was chilly now. When the Phantom breathed, he could see his breath in the air. He rubbed his hands together, working warmth into them. "But they don't have all three."

The Phantom hoped this would temporarily appease his father, but it was immediately obvious that it didn't.

"We don't know for sure, do we? We don't know how many they may have. In the wrong hands . . ." He shook his head. "Do you have any idea what it means if the Brotherhood gains control of the skulls?"

"Yes." He knew all too well. "They would be invincible."

Guran walked into the chamber. "Excuse me, Ghost Who Walks."

"Uh, yes . . . Guran."

He looked around curiously. "I thought I heard voices. Were you talking to somebody?"

The Phantom looked over at where his father had

stood; no one was there. The chill in the air had also vanished.

Sometimes after these unexpected encounters, the Phantom wondered if he had actually been talking to a ghost. Maybe it was all his imagination; his way of working things out. After all, Guran had never seen his father. Or if he had, he'd never mentioned it.

The only thing the Phantom knew for certain was that when he asked to see his father, demanded to see him, or asked for proof, his father never appeared. Then when he was certain that he'd never really been visited by him, the apparition would appear again.

"Only myself, Guran. I was talking to myself."

Zak lay on a pile of thick blankets inside the mouth of Skull Cave. The Phantom's home. His hideout. He'd heard that no one knew where it was, and now he was really here. This was the most exciting day of his life. Nothing like this had ever happened to him.

He would like to stay here and see all the great things that the Phantom could do. Maybe he could even help him. But how could he help Ghost Who Walks? He was just a kid and not a very big kid at that.

Then he felt the kerchief in his back pocket. His father's kerchief. No, he couldn't stay here. He had to get his father free from the bad men. Maybe Ghost Who Walks would help him. Zak was sure that he wanted to find out where the bad man named Quill had gone. And Zak suddenly realized that he knew where Quill would go. He would return to the ship where his father was being held captive.

*   *   *

The main street of Zavia was unpaved and lined with two-story wood-frame buildings that were, without exception, badly in need of paint. Most of them were gambling dens, houses of ill-repute, and bars. There were a couple of restaurants featuring Bangalla home cooking and a couple of places to buy supplies. Most of the buildings rented out rooms on the second floors.

The road slanted down a steep hill to the port with its long dock. There were a string of native huts along the shore and two dozen colorful fishing native boats. Occasionally foreign ships would dock here and sometimes hire new crew members from the town's sailors and ex-cons.

It was a squalid town, but it was a haven for outcasts. Nobody asked too many questions, and the closest thing to the law was the Sengh Brotherhood, who resolved all disputes by quick and often lethal means.

Quill limped up the long wooden sidewalk from the harbor to the center of town with his leather satchel over his shoulder. He was tired and bruised, but he was glad he was back in town, safe and alive, and carrying the ticket to his future. Now he just wanted to go to his room to recover and lay low for a while.

He had caught a ride to the port on a horse and wagon after he'd talked the Jungle Patrol into driving him to the main road. The officers were so astonished by the collapse of the bridge and his story about how it had happened that they hadn't even bothered asking him what he was doing out there. Quill had told them that the Phantom had shoved him out of his truck and driven it wildly onto the bridge, causing the collapse.

The Jungle Patrol rarely came much closer to Zavia than its outpost, headquartered a few kilometers outside the town. Off-duty patrolmen were warned to stay out of town for their own good. On rare occasions when they came into Zavia, it was usually to deal with a problem related to the tribal population. The *bonos* were left alone unless they made trouble with the tribal population, and even then the Brotherhood often intervened before the patrol arrived.

Now that he was back in Zavia his confidence was returning. After all, he'd not only found the silver skull and made it back to town with it, but he'd killed the Phantom. Again. That alone was cause for celebration. He also wanted to keep an eye out for Morgan and Breen. So instead of going to his room, he turned into one of his hangouts and ordered a whiskey at the bar.

By the time he ordered his second shot, he saw trouble coming his way in the form of a slender young woman with short hair, wearing pants. She wore a sleeveless white undershirt and an unbuttoned khaki jacket over it. He figured she was between twenty-five and thirty, but she had a mouth on her like an old sailor.

He nodded to her, grinned, and ordered her a drink. Like himself, she worked for Drax. He'd been hoping that connection would make her a willing companion, but so far she had a mind of her own.

"Hey there, Quill," she said, running a hand through her hair. She gave him a suspicious look.

"Haven't seen you around for a couple of days. Where you been?"

"Hiking in the jungle. Enjoying the scenery."

She laughed. "Yeah, sure. You hate this place. Why did you come back?"

"The same reason you're here. That's what the boss wanted."

She waved a hand. "I'm not his slave. I do what I want. I kind of like this rot-gut town."

He shook his head and laughed. He wanted to tell her about the crypt and the jewels and show her the skull, but he thought better of it. There were a half dozen guys at the bar within hearing range, so he decided to keep his thoughts about that matter to himself.

He swallowed his second shot in a single gulp. "I'm doing just fine, Sala. Just fine."

She looked him over. "You don't look like you've been doing just fine. You look like you've been playing in the mud, and you were limping when you walked in here a few minutes ago."

"I'm flattered that you noticed." After a moment, he added: "I had a little trouble out there in the jungle today."

"Oh, what kind of trouble?" she asked, leaning closer to him.

"Unexpected trouble. I ran into someone I killed about ten years ago. Killed him again today."

"Say what?"

He smiled as he thought about the story. While it was on his mind, it was a good opportunity to impress Sala, to get on her good side. "You ever heard of a strange guy named the Phantom?"

She frowned. "That's just some old native superstition, isn't it?"

"I used to think so, too. I thought the Phantom, the Ghost Who Walks, whatever they call him, was some kind of joke, just a stupid story about some masked man who was supposed to be hundreds of years old."

He rolled up his sleeve and displayed the Sengh Brotherhood logo. "But the Brotherhood wanted him dead, and when they send out an order, you carry it out without question."

"A small army began searching the deep jungle, half of them *bonos* out of Zavia, the rest were already part of the Brotherhood," he continued. "One by one the men started disappearing. Sometimes lions or leopards got them. Other times fights in camp ended in bloodshed. Still other times, there was no telling what had happened.

"One of the camp guards, a native, said he was sure that the Ghost Who Walks crept around the camp at night and was responsible for the disappearances. Whenever our numbers dipped too low, reinforcements were sent in. It went on like that for several weeks.

"Finally one day two of the toughest men who had the most jungle experience raced into camp. They'd found the Phantom's hideout, but before we could set out, a purple-clad giant charged into camp on a great white steed with a vicious wolf at his side. Some of the men were trampled, others were shot, and others were ripped apart by the wolf. Gunfire and smoke filled the air. The camp was in complete chaos.

"Then the wolf was chasing me, snapping at my

heels. I dove into the thicket, rolled over, and shot the wolf dead. It dropped in front of me, hanging over the limb of a tree. Blood was pouring from the wound in its forehead.''

He had her full attention now; she seemed fascinated by the story and he rushed on.

"Then I saw a flash of purple, and the Phantom leaped in and saw the wolf, saw me, and went mad. He aimed both his guns at me, but I was ready for him. I fired first and got him right between the eyes. It was great.''

"That's something," Sala said.

Quill nodded, and chewed on his cigar, pleased that she was taking a new look at him—as if she hadn't really seen him until now. "We even cut off his head and took it back to the boss as a prize trophy. There were only a few of us who survived.''

That was the story he liked to tell. He'd heard it from another member of the Brotherhood, an older man who claimed that he'd killed the Phantom twenty-five years earlier. The old man just couldn't understand how the Phantom could still be alive.

Quill had killed him, too, and he didn't understand, either. Only his story wasn't as exciting. He'd been attacked by a rabid monkey while panning for gold in a stream, and the Phantom had nursed him back to health in his hideout. In return Quill told him that he would show him where the Sengh hideout was located.

Quill was blindfolded before they left so that he wouldn't remember how to find the Phantom's Skull Cave. When they stopped and the Phantom removed the blindfold, Quill stabbed him in the back. Then he had taken the Phantom's gunbelt as proof. The

Brotherhood was grateful and made him a member. They'd wanted the Phantom dead because he was getting too close to unraveling their secrets. But Quill had never been able to find Skull Cave, which he was sure was filled with treasures.

"But you said you killed him again today. How could that be?" Sala asked.

"I don't know. Maybe it wasn't really him. Doesn't matter, he's dead. You want another drink?"

"Why don't we go up to your room and I'll take care of your injuries?"

Quill smiled. "I'll take a bottle of whiskey along to help clean out the cuts."

Just as he ordered the bottle, two uniformed men from the Jungle Patrol walked into the bar. Everyone turned and stared at them. One of them was the same chunky fellow who had given him a ride to the main road. He didn't recognize the other one. The men carefully looked over everyone in the place.

"We're looking for the guy who saw a truck go down in the gorge today," the skinny one said. No one moved, no one said a word. Quill figured they'd found Breen and Morgan. If they took him in for questioning, they'd find the skull and take it away from him.

The chunky guy looked right at Quill, then he turned to his partner. "Naw, he's not here, either. C'mon. Let's go on."

The two men turned and left.

The whiskey bottle arrived, and Sala put a hand on his arm. "Let's go," she said.

But Quill was still reeling from his near escape. He'd heard that the Brotherhood paid off some of the Jungle Patrol to protect their members. Maybe that was what happened. Then again, maybe the chunky one knew they were outgunned, and he'd decided to get reinforcements. If that was the case, he was in serious trouble.

He wasn't about to get caught off-guard relaxing with Sala. He shoved her arm away. "Here, it's all yours. I've got to go."

"What? Where are you going?"

He looked over his shoulder. "You could say I'm shipping out."

As he reached the door, the bottle skipped off his shoulder and smashed against the wall. Sala followed up her throw with a string of salty curses. He kept going. He would see her later.

Right now he just wanted to hide out in the old freighter that Drax had sent to Bangalla for backup. Besides, he needed to send a coded message to the boss and tell him the good news.

NINE

Long Island, New York

Diana Palmer groaned as she pulled into the long driveway leading up to the opulent estate. The English-style manor was brightly lit against the black sky, and the driveway was jammed with Lincolns, Packards, and a couple of Pierce-Arrows. Several chauffeurs lounged nearby, smoking and talking.

"Great, what's this all about?"

She stopped her Ford Woody, blocking the entrance to the driveway. "Hey, you can't park there, lady," someone yelled.

"You're right," she shouted back. She stomped hard on the gas pedal and drove around the cars and across the expansive lawn toward the mansion. She parked directly in front of the main entrance and killed the engine.

Instantly a butler in a tuxedo flew out the door, waving his arms like a penguin trying to fly. "Say now, I beg your pardon! You can't, you just can't park . . ."

Diana stepped out from the Woody and slammed the door. She was twenty-five, slender, and effortlessly beautiful. She wore an old red and black flannel shirt with a checkerboard pattern and khaki work pants. Her short hair looked as disheveled as her clothing.

The butler reassessed the situation. "Oh, Miss Palmer!" He dropped his arms to his sides and straightened his back. "I didn't realize. I'm sorry. I, uh . . . well, I didn't recognize you, ma'am."

Diana waved a hand. "Forget it, Falkmoore. I would've thrown me out, too, if I didn't know better." She opened the back of the Woody and started to pull out the suitcases and travel trunks.

"Welcome back, Miss Palmer. Here, please, let me help you with those things."

Diana glanced toward the house as she stepped back from the Woody. The sound of an orchestra filtered out through the open door. "Looks like I showed up on the wrong evening."

She walked inside, followed by Falkmoore, who carried some of her luggage. A cocktail party was in progress, and a string quartet played for about thirty guests. She recalled her twenty-third birthday party, when Tommy Dorsey had played after her first choice, Duke Ellington, had been unable to make the date.

She looked around quickly. You never knew who would show up at Mother's soirees. She'd acted in the movies in her younger years and still kept in touch with many of her old acquaintances. In the past couple of years, Diana had met Charlie Chaplin, Greta Garbo, Mae West, James Cagney, even Will Rogers and Dorothy Parker.

Lily Palmer, dressed in an expensive gown and

draped in jewelry, immediately hurried over to her. "Oh, Diana! I can't believe you're here!"

"Mother, you look absolutely stunning!"

Lily studied her daughter's appearance and shook her head in dismay. "Really, dear. Your clothes could be, hmm, well . . ."

"Don't worry, I'll change."

"Your timing really couldn't be worse. But how are you, anyway?"

Before Diana can answer, Lily turned away to smile and wave at a passing guest. Diana recognized the man from his picture, which was frequently in the newspaper. A politician . . . no, the police commissioner. She couldn't recall his name. He nodded to her and she smiled.

"I've contracted malaria, Mother," she said with a deadpan expression when the commissioner moved out of hearing range.

Lily turned back to her, smiling, her thoughts elsewhere. "That's nice."

"I thought you'd think so." She stifled a smile. "That's Alaska for you."

"Alaska? I thought you were in the Yucatan. Instead it was the Yukon?"

"Probably both."

Her mother waved a hand. "Well, I never have been able to keep track of your travel itinerary."

"Diana!"

A handsome, distinguished-looking man in his midfifties, his hair threaded with silver, beamed and kissed her on the cheek.

"Sorry, Uncle Dave. I didn't know you were having a party."

"Oh, it's nothing. Just the Palmer Foundation Dinner. I'm much happier to see you!" He looked her over. "So tell me about the Yukon."

"Oh, Dave," Lily interrupted. "It was cold. What more do you want to know?" She turned to her daughter. "Diana, I'll just never understand what all this traveling and exploring is about. What is it that you are looking for, anyway?"

Diana actually found her mother endearing, even though she had no idea what Diana's life was about. "I'm really not sure, Mother."

"Now look at that!" Uncle Dave exclaimed, his voice tight, his shoulders tensing as he turned toward the door. "Why in the world is Xander Drax here?"

Diana saw a commotion near the entrance as a tall, handsome man greeted friends loudly and shook hands. Heads turned and guests started to gravitate toward him.

"He made a very large contribution to the foundation," Lily confided.

"Return it," Uncle Dave replied.

"But he's a respected businessman."

"No," Uncle Dave said. "He's a thug."

Lily shrugged and turned to Diana. "Well, why don't you freshen up."

She exchanged a look of concern with Uncle Dave regarding Drax. "I think I'll get something to eat for now, Mother."

Lily placed a hand lightly on her shoulder and leaned toward her ear. "Jimmy Wells is here. I'm sure he'd love to see you."

"Oh, really," she said without enthusiasm. Uncle Dave winked at her. "I'm not sure Diana appreciates your matchmaking efforts, Lily."

"Oh, poo."

Diana smiled to herself and slipped into the kitchen. Caterers were busy preparing the main courses for the upcoming meal. She grabbed a plate and found a table with a variety of sliced cheeses and meats as well as breads, fruits, and pâtés. As she prepared a sandwich, she thought back on her recent trip.

One of the reasons she'd gone to Alaska and the Yukon was to get away from the persistent courting rituals of the Jimmy Bird, as she called him. There'd been no better place to avoid him than an Inuit village near the Arctic Circle, a place Jimmy wouldn't dream of going.

Diana collected folklore from the elders and, in fact, was compiling legends from primitive tribes all over the world. She was particularly intrigued by legends in which the usual separations between nature and humans were blurred. Human lovers became mountains, stars, and trees. A maiden marries a merman; a man weds the moon. But what really fascinated her was when ancient legends seemed to come alive in the present.

Her latest adventure began when an elderly medicine woman, who'd been avoiding her, finally invited Diana into her home. She prepared a cup of a soup, and Diana felt compelled to drink it, even though it tasted bitter and made her lips pucker. After Diana finished the soup, the woman told her a detailed and charming story about a whale who took a human wife.

As she listened to the old woman talking, Diana began to perspire and feel uneasy. Finally she excused herself and stepped outside. Even though there was only an hour of sunlight left, she decided to take a walk outside the village. She tromped off into the tundra, intending to return in a few minutes.

The sky and ground were almost an identical off-white tone, and the landscape was monotonously flat. But something compelled her to continue on. The soup, it seemed, had given her unexpected energy. A sense of well-being permeated her. She felt as if she could walk forever.

It was dusk when she realized she was lost, that she had no idea which way to go to return to the village. She suspected the old woman had fed her a narcotic of some kind. She'd lost control of her senses, and now she was starting to panic. If she didn't find her way back soon, she would freeze to death. Although she didn't feel the cold yet, she knew she would very soon.

She heard the crunching of snow . . . footsteps. It was coming from just over a rise to her left. Maybe some hunters from the village were on their way home or the old woman had put together a search party.

Diana rushed through the crispy snow, sinking to her ankles with each step. She gasped for breath as she reached the top of the rise and looked up into the fierce gaze of a ten-foot tall grizzly bear standing up on its hind legs.

The creature probably weighed six hundred pounds. Two quick steps and a swipe of its paw and Diana would never again see her family, and no one would know what happened to her. Slowly she dropped to her knees, then crouched down and rolled into a tight ball. She remained utterly still, tried to stay calm. She listened to the grizzly's raspy breath, squeezed her eyes shut. Her heart pounded in her ears.

After a couple of minutes, she slowly lifted her head. That was when she felt its paw on her shoulder. But it was a hand in a furry mitten, not a paw. A man crouched in front of her. His dark eyes searched her face as he helped her to her feet. She was so relieved that she started crying and hugged the man. He softly stroked her cheek and held her for a long time.

She told him about the grizzly, and he assured her the bear had gone. When she asked him if he knew the way to the village, he pointed with his chin and said that it smelled in that direction. As they began walking, she realized there was something peculiar about the man. She'd never seen him before, and knew that she was at his mercy in much the same way that she'd been at the bear's mercy.

Then she saw lights and smoke from the village. She thanked the man for his help, but he turned away when she asked if he was coming to the village with her. She watched him as he lumbered off. He seemed to grow in bulk and height and walk with an animal-like gait. His hooded fur coat molded around his body so that he looked like the grizzly. She heard a deep growl, and then he was lost in the darkness.

Diana felt a tug in her solar plexus and found herself on the floor of the medicine woman's hut. As she sat up, she felt drowsy and disoriented. She rubbed her arms and felt her hands. She wasn't even cold. "How did I get back here?"

To her astonishment, Ella said that she'd never left. Diana told her that she was certain that she'd been outside for at least a couple of hours.

"There is more than one way to travel, you know," Ella replied, then asked for an accounting of what had happened to her. After Diana had finished telling her story, Ella grinned and said that the grizzly bear had been a gentleman. "It's strange, but in the legends the animals often behave better than their human counterparts."

"Well, well, Diana. Welcome back home. What are you doing here all by yourself?"

She looked up, startled from her musings. Jimmy Wells leaned against the counter next to her in his tuxedo, martini in hand, watching her as she ate her sandwich. Jimmy's features were soft but attractive. To Diana he defined the expression "idle rich."

"Hi-ya, Jimmy Bird."

He smiled. "Keep up with that and I'll change it to Commander Byrd, and we'll fly off together to the North Pole."

If nothing else, Jimmy always had a quick comeback to her gentle prodding. "You'd hate the North Pole. You'd find it too cold."

He grinned. "Not with you there to keep me warm."

Diana avoided a reply; she didn't want to get him going. But Jimmy apparently wasn't finished.

"You know," he said, "I had the strangest urge a few weeks ago to charter a plane, track you down up there in the frozen North, charge into your hut, or tent, or log cabin, or whatever, sweep you off your feet, and bring you back here to New York."

"Really, Jimmy? Why didn't you?"

He shrugged. "I'm not sure exactly, but after a

few sets of tennis and a cold gin fizz, the urge just seemed to pass.''

She laughed. ''Immediate pleasures are so much more fun.''

Her sarcasm seemed to fly right over his head. He was looking her over, as if seeing her outfit for the first time. ''You look awfully pretty in those woodsy flannels. You must have been driving those poor lonely lumberjacks out of their minds.''

''I didn't see any lumberjacks.''

He moved closer to her. She was about to take a bite of her sandwich, but he pushed her arm down, cupped her chin in his palm, and kissed her on the mouth.

Diana didn't resist, but she didn't participate, either. When the kiss ended, her expression was completely passive. She barely resisted the urge to rub the back of her hand across her mouth.

He touched her chin with the tip of his finger, tilting her head upward, so she had to look at him. ''You have to admit, Diana, there's magic there.''

She simply took a big bite of her sandwich in response.

''What's in the sandwich?''

''Baloney,'' she replied.

TEN

As publisher of *The New York Tribune,* David Palmer often found himself socializing with people whose names and activities were the topic of articles in his paper, and they weren't always mentioned in the best light.

That made for some uncomfortable dealings, but Palmer was used to easing the hurt feelings of the town's politicians, celebrities, and assorted power brokers. On rare occasions, however, he spoke bluntly at social affairs, and tonight would be one of them.

Waiters were pushing carts laden with food, setting up the buffet, as he walked over to Mayor Krebs and Police Commissioner Farley. Both men were eyeing the ample buffet. He needed to talk with them, and he might as well get it over with before dinner. "Mayor. Commissioner. Are you enjoying yourselves this evening?"

"As much as I can in this monkey suit," Farley griped, tugging at the lapels of his tuxedo.

A waiter arrived with a fresh supply of cocktails. He picked up the empty glasses and moved on.

"Wonderful affair, Dave. You've outdone yourself," Krebs said jovially, and patted him on the back. He held up his drink. "To the Palmer Foundation and all such worthy causes."

"Thank you," Palmer said, clicking glasses. He was about to sip his drink when he glimpsed Xander Drax moving across the room toward the trio.

Drax extended a hand to Palmer and smiled congenially. "Now, here's the man I want to see!"

"You're not welcome here, Mr. Drax."

It wasn't Palmer's style to insult dinner guests, but in this case he intended to let Drax, as well as the mayor and police commissioner, know his exact sentiments. He found Drax's business dealings repugnant, and the last thing he wanted was for any of his guests to think he had invited him here.

Drax lowered his hand, his eyes narrowed, his jaw settled in a defiant pose. Then he smiled again. "I see the police commissioner is right here. Why don't you have me arrested?"

"Be sure to sample the buffet on your way out, Mr. Drax."

"For God's sake, Dave," Krebs interjected. "That isn't necessary."

"Thank you, Mayor, but I can speak for myself." A beat passed as Drax studied Palmer. "Dave, your reporters are poking their noses into my personal affairs and I don't understand why."

"You will. When we publish our story. And I assure you that you won't have to wait much longer, either. As you know, you've been given every opportunity to respond to the allegations."

"Why go after me?" Drax touched his hand to his chest, a gesture that seemed to say, *Why little ole harmless me?* "I'm just a private citizen."

"Private citizen?" Palmer could hardly contain

himself. "You own companies that regulate public utilities. You control the trade unions. You influence interest rates and stock prices. And you have personal and business involvement with the Zephro crime family. I'd say you were a very public figure, Mr. Drax."

Drax looked bemused. "In all my life, I've never heard such tall tales." He looked at Krebs and Farley as if for support. The two men smiled uneasily, uncertain how to react.

"Dave, have you been speaking to my ex-wives?" Drax asked. You know what I . . ." He turned to the mayor. "Mr. Krebs, how much does this newspaper cost?"

"Ten cents daily. Twenty cents on Sunday."

Drax laughed. "No, I mean all of it. The building, the presses, the typewriters. Maybe I'll just buy the whole thing."

Palmer could hardly believe what he was hearing. Drax was so used to buying his way out of trouble that he thought he could take over the paper. Palmer struggled to control his anger. "Not everything in life is for sale."

Drax was no longer amused. The tension was as thick as storm clouds. Lightning flashed in Drax's eyes. He leaned menacingly close to Palmer and spoke in a low voice that sounded like thunder. "I usually get what I want, Dave." Then with a big smile as if the sun had just broken through the clouds, he added: "You know, that buffet sounds good about now. Excuse me."

Drax moved off as Diana walked up to her uncle. "That arrogant—"

"Diana!" Palmer admonished.

"Dave, if you want my personal opinion, I think your newspaper should kill this investigation it's doing on Mr. Drax," Mayor Krebs said.

Farley nodded in agreement. "He's a rich and powerful man, and maybe he bends the rules once in awhile. But so what? There's no story there."

"That's the way I see it, too, Dave," Krebs said. "No story."

Palmer and Diana exchanged a look. He knew that Diana was thinking Krebs and Farley were acting like spineless pawns. But he wanted to give them the benefit of the doubt. "Mayor, Commissioner, I think we should talk in private. There are a few things you should know."

"Can I join you?" Diana asked.

He looked at the two men, who shrugged. "It's always nice to have a pretty girl sitting in on these tedious matters," Krebs said in a patronizing voice.

The truth was that Palmer considered Diana his confidant. He trusted her opinions, and he was pleased to see that she had not only quickly recognized the importance of the situation, but that she was interested in helping him. They moved down a long hallway, through the smoking room and into the library, where Palmer sat down at his desk. Diana remained standing to one side as Krebs and Farley took seats opposite Palmer.

"Gentlemen, I have learned from a highly placed source at the city library that Xander Drax has been conducting extensive research using a number of esoteric volumes that are normally kept under constant lock and key."

Krebs turned his palms up. "So?"

Palmer took out an envelope from his file folder

and handed it to the mayor. "He's interested in something connected with this symbol."

Krebs opened the envelope and looked impassively at the paper inside, which contained a stylized spider-web design. Krebs shrugged, then handed the envelope to Farley.

"So, what's it mean?" Krebs asked. It was evident in his voice that he thought Palmer was wasting his time.

"It means that Drax is tampering with the darkest forces of evil." Palmer paused; the remark hung like smoke in the air. "He's on a quest for a nefarious supernatural power. That much we know. In his hands, nothing good can come of it."

Krebs and Farley exchanged a look. Even Diana was startled by this news. "We're not sure exactly what you mean," Farley said.

"These are perilous and turbulent times," Palmer continued. "Dictators and tyrants are popping up all over. Drax already has the desire to become one himself, and this supernatural power will provide him with the means to achieve his goal."

"Nonsense," Krebs scoffed.

"I know. It's hard to fathom," Palmer said. "But Drax believes in it, and this man *must* be taken seriously. Everything we've learned about him suggests that he is a dangerous megalomaniac."

Diana moved closer to him and looked at the contents of the file that was open on his desk. She probably noticed the airline ticket and was wondering where he was going. "I've been able to trace the origin of that spider-web symbol to the infamous Bangalla jungle, one of the world's last frontiers. And somewhere in that jungle is the supernatural power that Drax wants more than anything else in this world.''

Diana snatched up the airline ticket. ''This is a ticket for the Pan Am Clipper. You're not thinking of going into the Bangalla jungle, are you?''

Palmer closed the file folder. ''I leave tomorrow. I'm meeting a man named Captain Philip Horton. I've got to get to the bottom of this.'' Turning to the mayor and police commissioner, he added, ''I can promise you both that there will be no article until I've found out exactly what Drax is after and what this spider-web symbol means.''

''You can't turn your back on Drax that long,'' Diana said. ''You need to stay here and take care of things. I don't think you should go.''

''Listen to your niece, Dave,'' Krebs said. ''She's right, of course. The jungle is no place for a man your age. You have other responsibilities.''

''Probably just a wild goose chase, anyway,'' Farley added.

''Let me go for you,'' Diana said.

Krebs and Farley did a double take. ''You can't be serious,'' Krebs said.

''You, Diana?'' Palmer didn't doubt that she was serious about her offer, but he didn't feel right imposing on her. ''But you just got home. You've probably got a lot of things to do.''

''I have nothing pending that's more important,'' she said firmly. ''Besides, I'm getting restless already. I want to go.''

Palmer raised his eyes toward the ceiling. ''Your mother will have a fit.''

Diana smiled. ''We've never let that bother us before, Uncle Dave.''

Palmer thought she was probably referring to the time he'd sent her to the Amazon to track down a missing scientist who was collecting native plants used by shamans to cure illnesses. She'd returned with the man's head shrunken to the size of a fist. It made a great story, but Lily hadn't spoken to him for two weeks.

Or maybe Diana was thinking of the Five Treasures of the Snow incident. The two of them had joined an expedition to the world's third highest peak, located in the Himalayas between Nepal and Sikkim—Mount Kinchinjunga, which means Five Treasures of the Snow because its summit consisted of five peaks.

Palmer had climbed as far as the base camp, but Diana had continued on with five others. They were on the last leg to the top of one of the peaks when they were caught in a midsummer snowstorm.

Diana and one of the men were the only ones to survive and find their way back to the base camp three days later. Palmer didn't think that Lily had ever forgiven him for allowing Diana to try to reach the summit.

For that matter, she had never forgiven him for allowing Diana to accompany him on the expedition. This would just be one more black mark against him.

"I think we can work something out," he said.

He turned to Krebs and Farley. "Can I trust you both to keep the lid on this discussion? We certainly don't need anyone else knowing what we've talked about."

"Oh, of course not," Krebs said.

"You have my word," Farley chimed in.

ELEVEN

The black Packard, one of Drax's newer cars, was parked in the usual meeting place near the harbor. The headlights were turned on, illuminating the ground fog that was rolling over the desolate dock area.

He'd been so preoccupied with his quest, he hadn't taken the *Tribune*'s investigation seriously. He'd assumed that Palmer would withdraw his reporters once he realized Drax's displeasure. Now he knew that Palmer was an idealistic type who thought he was doing the city a favor by exposing him.

But Drax certainly wasn't about to sit back and allow his life to be picked apart in the newspaper. Especially not now. Nothing could disrupt his plans. The first thing he needed to know, though, was how much Palmer had found out.

After tonight's encounter, he suspected the worse. But once he knew for sure, he would figure out the best way to deal with the newspaper publisher.

In the distance, a pair of lights moved slowly through the soupy darkness. The lights brightened until they stopped directly in front of the Packard. Then they dimmed and vanished, as if the darkness had swallowed them.

The hazy outline of a Ford came into view. The front door opened and Police Commissioner Jack Farley stepped out. He hoisted his slacks as he hastened over to the Packard.

Drax unlocked the back door and Farley slipped into the car. "Thanks for coming on such short notice," Drax said.

Without preface, Farley replied, "Well, you were right. They know far too much."

"How much?"

"More than you'd like."

"Spell it out," Drax snapped impatiently.

For the next ten minutes, Drax listened to Farley with a swelling sense of doom and rage. He asked several questions and each time he heard the commissioner's replies, his body tensed.

"Anything else, Mr. Drax?" Farley asked when Drax didn't say anything.

Drax barely heard him. He was staring straight ahead, deep in concentration as he formed his plans.

Drax moved across his expansive office, his feet sinking into a carpeting so thick that it was like walking on an immense sponge.

The office was a glass cave high above the city. Everything Drax needed was here or a phone call away. He stopped at the window and stared out over the New York skyline, admiring the skyscrapers.

His power here was already enormous. *But just wait,* he thought. *Just wait. They ain't seen nothing.* He laughed to himself, then turned away as the phone rang. He strolled over to his desk.

"Drax here."

"It's Ray Zephro. Our little tootsie is boarding the

plane right now. Just say the word and I'll have her dragged off by her hair.''

''Hello, Ray. How is your little brother, Charlie, doing?''

''He's doing just fine, Xander. Just fine. We're a little short on time here. What do you say? I need to know now.''

Sitting back in his comfortable leather chair, Drax absentmindedly played with a specially designed binocular microscope. When he adjusted the focus, a pair of razorlike spikes popped out from the dual eyepieces. Drax touched the tip of his index finger to one of the spikes and smiled. *Painful and quite lethal,* he thought.

''Xander, you there?''

''Yeah, I'm here. Thanks just the same, Ray, but I have another way of dealing with this. After all, I do have friends in that part of the world.'' The girl's disappearance in the jungle would cause far less commotion than a public kidnapping in her hometown. ''I've got to go. Dr. Fleming is here.''

''Who?''

''The librarian.''

Drax hung up the phone, set the microscope down, then touched the intercom. ''Alice, send in Dr. Fleming, please.''

A moment later, the door opened and a tall man with an aristocratic bearing moved confidently into the room. Self-assured, even smug, he didn't seem a bit intimidated by Drax's urgent request for a meeting. If Drax's power and reputation worried him, he didn't show it.

''Thank you for coming on such short notice, Dr. Fleming.''

Fleming took a seat in a comfortable chair, crossed his legs, and folded his hands together. "I don't mind. It's a nice day for a walk. How can I help you?"

Drax leaned forward and ran a finger down the length of the microscope. He studied Fleming a moment before he spoke. "You can assure me that the research I've been doing at the city library is strictly confidential."

"Of course it is."

Drax nodded thoughtfully. "Are you sure? Because Dave Palmer has been poking his nose into my business of late." He paused, allowing his words to impact Fleming, and scrutinized him without appearing to do so. "I'm sure you know Mr. Palmer is the publisher of the *Tribune*."

Fleming adjusted his position in the chair. *Slightly nervous now,* Drax thought.

"Of course I know that. And you have nothing to worry about, Mr. Drax. Your privacy is protected. All requests for access to special collections come directly to me. I'm the only one who sees them."

"Thanks. I feel a lot better now. You see, I would be very upset if my activities were being discussed. I just hate gossip, you know."

"Oh, I understand. Nothing to worry about," Fleming assured him.

"One more thing, if you don't mind. I'd like your professional opinion on something under this microscope." Drax pushed it across the desk. "Here. Let me hold your glasses."

Fleming looked mildly surprised by the request. "I'm no expert on the microscopic world, you know." Nonetheless, he moved over to the microscope. He removed his glasses and peered through the dual eyepieces. "What is it I'm supposed to be looking at? I don't see anything."

"Turn the focus knob."

Drax knew that the word LIAR would be coming into focus, then Fleming would have one second before the spring was triggered. Fittingly, it would be the last thing Fleming ever saw.

"Perhaps I should do it with my glasses on," Fleming murmured, and reached for his glasses.

Drax pushed them aside before he touched them. "You'll be able to see better without them. Just adjust the focus knob."

A click.

The spikes shot through the eyepieces, piercing Fleming's pupils. He screamed, ripped the microscope away from his head, and covered his eyes with his hands. Blood poured through his fingers and he stumbled back, reeling in pain.

"You won't be needing these any longer." Standing up, Drax snapped Fleming's glasses in two pieces, then touched the intercom. "Alice, send the boys in, will you please? We have a little problem here."

The door opened and two beefy men in black suits and hats rushed into the room and took Fleming by the arms. He swung his head from side to side and kept shrieking, "Help me! Help me!"

A third man of similar proportions to the other two hurried into the room and quickly wrapped a bandage around Fleming's head, covering his eyes. Then he stuffed a gag into his mouth.

"Good work," Drax said. "Take care of him. You know what to do."

No one would see Fleming again. His disappearance would probably be a much discussed mystery in the *Tribune*, Drax thought, and smiled as he sat back down. He looked at the bloody spikes sticking through the top of the eyepieces. Maybe one day he'd tell Palmer what happened to him, before Palmer did his own disappearing act.

TWELVE

The Sea of Bangalla

The flight from New York was long and tedious and was now stretching into its third day. Diana Palmer had switched planes twice and had stopped four times. Or was it five? She could no longer remember. It didn't matter. She was almost to her destination now; another hour or so to go.

In the early years of her travels, it had taken her days to recover from a trip of this duration. She had yearned for hot showers, a hot meal, a soft bed, creature comforts. But then she'd started traveling with Uncle Dave and such comforts had come to seem frivolous, beside the point. Now all she needed was a short nap to revive herself before they landed.

She shifted to face the window and closed her eyes. She'd slept off and on, but never for more than three hours at a time.

She was hoping that she would be able to deal quickly with her uncle's business. She'd find out whatever she could about the spider-web symbol and try to discover exactly what Drax was up to.

Uncle Dave had cautioned her not to get directly involved, but to simply gather information and get out as soon as possible. The more that they knew, the better Drax's plans could be combated.

Diana agreed, but she also wanted to take advantage of another opportunity that presented itself. She would be able to get close to some of the Bangalla tribes, which had never been subjugated by foreign colonists.

Some of the mysterious tribes had gained considerable notoriety for their pirateering activities, especially in the seventeenth and eighteenth centuries. In fact, the English had adapted the name Bangallamen, so that it no longer referred to native people as much as to creatures in the night that every child feared. She herself had grown up fearing the Bangallamen, having no idea of the source of the name.

But she'd also heard that the Bangallans' reputation was not exactly all that the history books described. They were known to attack foreign ships entering their territory and supposedly possessed unusual navigational skills. But that alone didn't mean they were responsible for all of the vicious attacks through which they'd gained their notoriety. Diana hoped to learn the legends and the true history of the tribes before returning to the States.

The plane suddenly jerked, nearly tossing her out of her seat. The wing outside her window dipped down, lifted, dipped again. What was going on? A chorus of startled shouts rose from the passengers.

She peered out the window into the darkness and saw stars and the moon. As far as she knew, there had been no adverse weather conditions expected for the rest of the flight.

Then she glimpsed lights just above the aircraft and saw the outline of a fighter plane with pontoons. What was it doing so close to the plane? Her stomach lurched, she pressed her hands to the back of the seat in front of her and the plane's nose suddenly plunged downward. The craft dropped hundreds of feet in a matter of seconds.

Diana gasped for air, trying to catch her breath. Passengers cried out, someone shouted for help, a stewardess fell in the aisle. She managed to look out the window again, and this time she saw fighter planes sweep in formation past the Clipper.

"We are experiencing some difficulties in our flight path," the pilot said over the intercom. "Please make sure your seat belts are fastened properly and bear with us. We apologize for any inconvenience."

The fighter planes repeated their aggressive maneuvers, dipping down toward the plane, darting dangerously close to it as the Clipper continued to descend. There was no doubt in Diana's mind that they were being forced to land. But she was fairly certain there was no airport, nor land of any kind, below them.

Her first concern was her immediate survival. But other questions lingered in the back of her mind. Why, she wondered, were they being forced down, and could it somehow be related to her own mission? Did Drax have that kind of power? Would he take such a large risk?

She had the feeling the answer was yes.

*   *   *

The Phantom had been looking all over Skull Cave for Guran when he finally found him in the Radio Room. He wore a headset and was sitting in front of a vast array of radio equipment that was notched into the cave's rock walls. Unaware that the Phantom had entered the room, Guran adjusted a couple of dials and hastily cranked the handle on the generator.

"Guran?"

The Phantom raised his voice above the buzzing and crackling of tubes and transistors, but Guran didn't respond. Beside him, Zak, the native kid who the Phantom had saved from the truck, looked around in awe at all the complicated equipment.

The Phantom reached out and removed the headset. Startled, Guran spun around. "Oh, you!"

"Who did you expect?"

"You startled me."

"Sorry. Zak and I are leaving. He says the men who stole the skull came from a ship docked in a hidden cove on the other side of the jungle. He thinks he can find it. It's worth a shot." He held up the headset. "What are you listening to, 'Junior G-Men'?"

"I wish it was," Guran said. "This is real. Go ahead, listen."

The Phantom put the headset to his ears and heard the sound of urgent voices. "I repeat: This is the Pan Am Clipper. We are under attack ... under attack by three fighter planes. We are down about five miles off the Bangalla coast. We are taking on water."

Static disrupted the transmission and the Phantom lowered the headset. "The Pan Am Clipper has been forced down over the ocean.'' He was quiet a moment, then turned to Zak. ''Wait here with Guran. I'll be back in a little while.''

The Phantom moved out into the main chamber of the cave and sat down on the majestic Skull Throne. Raised above the floor and decorated with skull designs, the high-backed throne was hundreds of years old. It had been a gift to the Phantom from an Arab prince, but the story of what the Phantom had done to deserve the gift had been forgotten long ago. It was a part of his heritage that had never been recorded.

He mounted the throne and relaxed. Closing his eyes, he willed himself to the site of the downed plane. Then he focused his attention on his breath and released his thoughts.

Slowly he became more and more relaxed, until he was drifting on the border of sleep. Then his uncanny navigational skills, which he'd learned from his father, took effect. He didn't know how he found his way to places with his mind, but the radio contact was all he needed to locate the Pan Am Clipper.

The landscape below him blurred as he moved at lightning speed toward his objective. Then the jungle was gone and the ocean glistened in the moonlight below him. Ships came into view and vanished, and then he saw the airplane bobbing on the waves. A small fighter plane on pontoons was approaching the Clipper, water shooting out from behind it in a fine, moonlit spray.

Inside the plane, stewardesses tried to calm the frightened passengers, but they were on the verge of panic themselves. The Phantom wished he could do something to help them, but he was powerless to act.

Inside the fighter plane were three men dressed in coverall flight suits with parachutes strapped to their backs. They wore goggles and caps. One of them was armed with a machine gun, and another was talking on the radio to the captain of the Clipper. His message was clear: they were coming aboard, and if there was any resistance, the plane would be shot apart and sunk by the two other fighters still in the air. The captain of the Clipper replied that he was sorry, but the door was jammed. They couldn't get it open.

For an instant, the man looked up, frowning. Then he spoke to the captain again. ''We're coming aboard right now. Open that door or we'll blow it off.''

The Phantom blinked open his eyes. He felt the throne beneath him and looked around the skull chamber. He took in a deep breath, exhaled, and leaped down from the throne.

Was there time? Could he make it to the Clipper before it was blown to smithereens? Maybe.

He bolted out of the cave, Zak hurrying to catch up.

The fighter plane was nestled right under the wing outside Diana's window. It was linked to the Clipper by a rope, and now in the murky darkness, a raft was crossing the short span between the two planes.

She pressed closer to the window, trying to see the occupants of the raft. She could only make out vague forms, but it was enough to leave her with a distinct sense of foreboding.

Other passengers had also seen the raft, but in the confusion some of the passengers thought the fighter ship was there to rescue them from the sinking craft. A man in the row in front of her hailed a passing stewardess. "How are we all going to fit onto that raft? Aren't there any ships in the area that can help?"

The stewardess leaned toward him, her face pale, her expression betraying her fear despite her attempts to keep it masked from the passengers. "We're doing all we can to deal with this situation, sir. Please put on your life vest. As soon as a ship arrives, we'll all be taken aboard. There's really nothing to worry about."

Sure, Diana thought. Things were bad and were going to get a lot worse.

Suddenly the chatter of machine guns shredded the air. Passengers screamed and dived for cover. Diana quickly slipped the envelope containing the Sengh Brotherhood symbol from her pocket and pushed it down inside her boot.

She smelled sea air seeping into the cabin. The door to the Clipper swung open, three men scrambled inside. One carried the machine gun that had just ripped apart the lock on the door. The other two brandished side arms. Their caps and goggles hid their faces.

One of the men pointed at a cowering old man. "He'll do."

A second flyer grabbed the man and aimed the machine gun at his chest. People screamed, blood drained from the old man's face.

"We want Diana Palmer," said the first flyer, who apparently was the leader. "And we're prepared to kill all of you, one by one, until she steps forward."

Panic spread through the cabin. The plane was rocking violently in the waves. "Who is she?" someone shouted.

"We don't know her."

"Maybe she's not here."

"We didn't do anything."

Diana stood up, her knees soft, a hole a mile wide tearing open in her stomach. "I'm Diana Palmer."

"So quickly? How disappointing," the first flyer scoffed.

"What do you want?" Diana asked.

"The pleasure of your company."

"Who are you?"

"That's none of your . . ."

Something about the voice and the look of the intruder roused her suspicion. Boldly, she reached out and yanked off the flyer's cap and goggles. It was a young woman, an aviatrix who could pass for Amelia Earhart's younger sister.

"Happy now, Diana Palmer? Get a good look? I suppose you want my name, too?"

"Sala," one of the men yelled, inadvertently providing the name. "The plane's going to sink. Let's get out of here!"

"One more thing," Sala said.

With that, she turned and struck Diana across the side of her head with the barrel of the pistol. She slumped to the floor. "Too bad. Now we've got to carry you out of here."

THIRTEEN

Captain Philip Horton was ready to retire for the evening after a long day at the Jungle Patrol outpost. He looked into the radio control room where Corporal Weeks was stationed.

"I'm going to turn in, Weeks. Wake me if there's any news."

"Yes, sir. But it's probably not going to be good news."

Horton agreed, but to Weeks he said, "Maybe our luck will turn."

"Maybe, Captain."

He didn't sound any more convinced than Horton was. They didn't need just luck; they needed a miracle.

Horton left the building and plodded back to his office. It doubled as his sleeping quarters and was hardly the picture of comfort. But hell, it was home.

He climbed the steps to the porch, stretched his arms and yawned. He and Weeks had been monitoring dramatic events at sea for the last several hours. The radio transmissions about the forced landing and its mysterious perpetrators were definitely the most startling transmission they'd received in months.

There was nothing more he could do. The passengers had all been rescued, except one woman, and Horton was particularly concerned about her, since she had been on her way to see him. Now he wondered if he would ever meet her.

Following the reports also took his mind off the local matter of the destroyed bridge and the missing witness who swore that the Phantom had fallen into the gorge with the truck. But there was no trace of the Phantom, as he'd suspected would be the case, and the witness, unfortunately, had not yet been found and probably never would be.

Once inside his office, Horton took off his gunbelt and unbuttoned his shirt. He splashed water on his face from a wash bowl, rubbed his hands vigorously over his face, and wondered what the hell he was going to do about the situation with the Clipper. As he reached for a towel, he glanced in the mirror and glimpsed movement. Horton spun around and sucked in his breath. His eyes locked with the Phantom's.

"Hey, can't you ever come in through the front door?" Horton snapped.

"Too obvious. I prefer the window."

Horton smiled and shook hands with the Phantom. "It's good to see you, Ghost Who Walks. I was getting worried when I found out about the bridge collapsing. I heard you were in that truck."

"Oh, that." He touched his side, which was nearly healed from the stab wound. "It's not the reason I came here."

"Let me guess." If there was trouble anywhere near Bangalla, the Phantom often found his way into the mess. "We've had some trouble tonight offshore."

"I know. I picked up the distress call on the radio. Any word?"

"The passengers were picked up by a Portuguese fishing boat," Horton said. "Everyone's safe . . . except a young woman abducted off the Clipper."

"Who?"

Horton's shoulders slumped. "She was on her way to meet me, oddly enough. Her name is Diana Palmer."

The Phantom reacted to the name. "Diana Palmer of New York? Her uncle owns the *Tribune*."

"Yeah, that's right." The Phantom obviously got away from the jungle from time to time. "How did you know her, if I may ask?"

The Phantom shrugged. "Maybe I heard the name somewhere, sounded familiar."

"First those grave robbers, and now this," Horton said. "Do you think the Sengh Brotherhood is involved in this airplane matter?"

"Good question. But why would they kidnap a young woman from New York?"

"I haven't a clue. I just hope we can get her back," Horton said.

"I'll see what I can do." The Phantom eyed the door as though he were about to leave.

But Horton wasn't ready for him to leave yet. "Your father had a theory about all this, you know."

Mention of his father caught the Phantom's attention, just as Horton had known it would. "What do you mean?"

Horton paced across the room. "He was certain the Sengh Brotherhood had a secret stronghold where they've been hiding for centuries."

"I know."

"He was never able to find it," Horton continued

as if the Phantom didn't already know. "He thought they had some kind of power to block him."

"Yeah. But he was getting close. When they realized it, they turned on him and he died." The Phantom reached for the doorknob. "I better get going."

Horton grabbed his arm. "Wait. Don't use the door. Go out the way you came in. I have enough trouble pretending you're not real as it is."

The Phantom looked amused. "Captain Horton and his double life." Then he climbed through the window and disappeared into the darkness.

The Phantom slipped away from the Jungle Patrol outpost and into the forest. Zak was patiently waiting for him, holding Hero's reins in one hand and his father's red and blue kerchief in the other. Nearby, Devil paced anxiously about, wary about being so near the outpost. The Phantom swung his leg over the white steed, then pulled Zak up behind him.

"Ghost Who Walks, I remember now. They had airplanes," Zak said.

For a moment, the Phantom wasn't sure who he was talking about. "You mean the men who tied you up in the truck? The bad men?"

"Yes. Planes with boats for feet."

The Phantom nodded. "Seaplanes." And fighter planes with pontoons had forced the Pan Am Clipper into the water. No coincidence there, he thought.

He reined Hero around and galloped off into the jungle with Devil, the wolf, running at his side. "Hang on, Zak. We've got a long ride ahead."

* * *

The last thing Diana remembered was being pistol-whipped by the woman from the fighter plane. Now, as she came awake, she was being lifted by rope up through the darkness. Her legs and wrists were bound and a wad of cloth was stuffed into her mouth. It smelled of dirt and oil. Her body slammed several times against the barnacle-encrusted piling as she was lifted to a dock. Then they dragged her along it for several yards.

"Stop right there, you idiot," Sala yelled at whoever was pulling Diana.

Sala loosened the rope under Diana's arms, slipped it over her head. Then she lifted Diana and carried her up a gangplank and onto the deck of an old freighter. From there she was dragged to an opening in the deck that led down into the belly of the ship.

As Sala let her go, Diana was suddenly afraid she was going to be shoved headfirst down the hole, and there was nothing she could do about it. She yelled into the gag, shook her head, and pulled her knees tightly into her chest.

"Take it easy. I'm not going to dump you."

Sala descended several steps, then draped Diana over her shoulder as though she weighed nothing at all. Diana stared helplessly down into the dank hold of the ship as Sala continued on. The musty air seeped into her nostrils, nauseating her.

When they finally reached the bottom, Sala carried her a few more yards, then deposited her in a wooden chair.

A seedy, roughneck character strolled casually over to Sala, who looked as if she were about to collapse from the effort. "What's your problem?"

"Thanks for all your help, Quill," Sala snapped.

"You might as well have stayed in town with your idiot friends."

Quill laughed; his teeth looked as if they hadn't been brushed in decades. "I've been getting a new image." He turned his cheek toward her. "What do you think?"

A skull tattoo now decorated each of the man's cheeks.

"You look just as ugly as the last time I saw you," Sala said.

"No, look! Matching skulls."

Sala fixed a hand to her waist and tilted sideways, stretching fatigued muscles. "What's the occasion? Did you kill your mother?"

"I'll never tell." He abruptly turned to Diana. "So let's see her mug."

Sala untied the dirty rag used for a gag. Diana spit bits of it out of her mouth. "Sort of pretty, I guess," Sala observed. "In a spoiled, rich girl kind of way. Definitely too classy for you."

"Oh, I don't know," Quill murmured, walking around her, eyeing her the way a butcher eyes a piece of prime beef. "You can never tell."

Diana cleared her throat. Her mouth felt like cotton, but she tried to talk, anyway. "Who are you people? Are you crazy?" Her voice croaked, the words sputtered out of her. "Do you have any idea how many laws you've just broken? Disruption of international air transportation! Abduction! Piracy! Kidnapping!"

Sala laughed. "Little Miss Righteous. Not your type at all, Quill."

Quill stepped closer to Diana and raised his arm,

threatening to strike Diana. "Shut up! Just shut the hell up!"

But Diana wasn't about to follow any orders from Tattoo Face. "If this is a kidnapping for money, you're not going to get a cent! Not a red cent!"

Quill turned to Sala. "Do you want to shut her up, or should I do it?"

Sala went over to Diana to replace the gag, but Diana jerked her head to the side. "Get that out of here. That rag is filthy! You wanna gag me ... get a clean rag! Is that too much to ask?"

Sala grabbed her by the jaw and finally jammed the rag back into her mouth.

"Somebody very important has a big interest in you, lady," Quill said. "I've got to report in now. When I get back, maybe we can enjoy some time alone. Just you and me." Quill pinched her cheek, then walked away. Sala laughed and followed him.

Diana shuddered and closed her eyes. *Think, and do it fast. You've got to get outta here.*

Just before dawn, the Phantom and Zak reached the edge of the jungle and dismounted. They traveled a short distance on foot, Devil close behind them. Crouching behind a large rock, they looked out onto a cove as the first gray light of dawn spilled across the water.

A long wooden dock extended out from a cluster of shacks and small buildings. A truck was parked nearby along with some horses hitched to a tree. But the Phantom's gaze was immediately drawn to the two seaplanes that bobbed in the water next to the dock. Beyond them, anchored near the end of the dock, was an old freighter like the ones he'd seen on occasion in the port of Zavia.

The Phantom touched Zak's shoulder. "You did good, Zak. Real good. Any idea how long that ship's been docked here?"

He shook his head. "I only saw it when the bad men took my father here."

"You better go back to your people, and stay away from the bad guys."

"What about my papa? Will you help him?" Zak's eyes filled with the nakedness of his plea.

"I'll do all I can, Zak. If I find him in there, I'll get him out. But I'm looking for a woman, too."

The Phantom called Devil, who loped over to his side. Kneeling down, the Phantom whispered in his ear. The wolf trotted over to the dock, then darted between the barrels and cargo boxes to avoid being seen. Finally he made a wild dash to the end of the dock, ran up the gangplank and onto the deck of the freighter.

"Good job," the Phantom said, then dove into the cool water. He swam just below the surface, coming up only once for air before he reached the starboard side of the freighter.

Crew members were loitering on the deck as the Phantom climbed up the anchor chain. He was several feet below the deck when he slipped through an open porthole and tumbled into the ship. He landed on a bunk bed, one that was occupied.

"Hey, what's going on here?" a bearded man grumbled as he sat up and found a dripping wet, purple-hooded masked man straddling him. The man's eyes bulged. "What on earth are you?"

"I'm a who, not a what."

"Spider Man?"

"Wrong."

The Phantom grabbed the man's head and slammed it against an iron pole at the corner of the bunk. "Sweet dreams."

He placed the unconscious man's head back on his pillow and crawled off the bed. He looked around the tight crew quarters. Sailors were sleeping in the other bunk beds, apparently undisturbed by the momentary ruckus.

The Phantom opened a door and entered a narrow corridor. He heard someone coming down a stairway to his immediate right. He turned left. A door swung open ten feet down the corridor. He reached back to the handle of the door he'd just closed.

Locked. He was trapped.

Then he saw another door across the hall. He reached for the handle, pulled, and it opened. He ducked inside just in time to avoid a confrontation in the corridor. He was in another section of crew quarters. It was empty.

He noticed a pair of flyer's goggles and a leather cap hanging from a post of an empty bunk bed. Nearby, strewn on a couple of bunks, were flight suits and more goggles. The Phantom heard the slamming of locker doors and shower water running in an adjoining room. He moved soundlessly in that direction.

If the flyers who had captured Diana Palmer were here, the Phantom might persuade one of them to lead him to her. He pulled out one of his pistols, which was a greater persuader, and opened the door. He was met by a haze of steam.

"Okay, nobody move, gentlemahh . . ."

The Phantom didn't finish the word. Five women in various stages of undress were in front of him. Several of them grabbed towels and covered themselves. The others just gaped for a few seconds, and so did the Phantom.

"Ah, sorry, ladies," he said, breaking the stunned silence. He holstered his gun. "I hope you'll pardon my error."

One of the women pulled a revolver from her locker and took a shot at him. The bullet pinged off a water pipe next to his head. "I guess not."

Before she got off another shot, the Phantom leaped feet first into a laundry chute and tumbled out onto a pile of clothing. "Interesting crew," he muttered.

FOURTEEN

Zak wandered along the dock, a fishing pole over his shoulder. Villagers came here every day to fish and no one would pay any attention to another kid with apparently the same intent.

He had cut the pole from the bamboo thicket a short distance away. It looked like an ordinary fishing pole, except it didn't have line with it. But then, Zak wasn't going fishing, either.

As he strolled past the gangplank leading to the freighter, he looked around the deck. There were only two crew members in sight. They were talking to each other and had their backs to the gangplank. He stopped, checked the immediate area to make sure no one was watching, then tossed the pole aside and stole up the gangplank.

He raced across the deck to the bulwark, pressed his back up against it. His heart pounded, and his breath came in short, startled gasps. It would be bad enough if he were caught here, but worse if the bad guys recognized him. He had to help Ghost Who Walks find his father, though. If he did nothing else with his life, he would do this.

Zak had always believed in Ghost Who Walks.

He'd heard stories all his life about the great things he did. How he helped people who were in trouble and how he'd been doing it since the olden times, long before anyone could remember.

His father assured him the stories were real, because his own father and grandfather remembered Ghost Who Walks, and Grandfather even said that *his* grandfather had once helped the Phantom fight off a dozen men who wanted to kill his daughter because they thought she was a witch.

When Zak had asked if the woman really was a witch, his grandfather had told him that she could see things in the future, and one of the things she saw was that Ghost Who Walks would be around for a long, long time.

Now he knew the witch was right and that Ghost Who Walks wasn't just an old story. Ever since they had escaped from the falling bridge, he could hardly contain himself. He couldn't wait to tell his friends how they had flown through the air as the bridge and truck disappeared into the gorge. Or how they had ridden on Hero, the white stallion who appeared out of nowhere every time the Phantom whistled for him.

He wanted to tell his friends everything. But he'd promised Ghost Who Walks that he would never say a word about being in Skull Cave. Besides, his friends would never believe him. Nobody went with Ghost Who Walks to Skull Cave.

Zak heard footsteps. Someone was coming his way. He slid along the bulwark, trying to stay out of sight. He slipped into a dark alcove and crouched down, pulling his knees in to his chest. He sniffed. Hot, stale breath.

Slowly he turned his head and saw large, glowing

green eyes staring at him from less than a foot away. He sucked in his breath and stifled a cry as he saw the snout and long sharp teeth. Then, as his eyes adjusted to the dim light, he realized it was Devil, the Phantom's huge wolf.

Two crew members walked by, passing within three feet of Zak. "What are you doing here, boy?" he whispered to the wolf. "You really scared me there." The wolf nudged his arm with its nose. "I'm glad you're on my side. I've got to find my papa. I think he's here."

Devil made a low growling sound, then took Zak's hand lightly in his jaws.

"What are you saying, boy? You want to help?" He remembered his father's kerchief and took it from his pocket. The wolf sniffed it, made a low whimpering sound, then scratched at the deck.

"Below deck? Let's go. Lead the way."

As the minutes ticked by in the dark hold of the freighter, Diana kept thinking about what might happen when Tattoo Face came back. She couldn't think of anything worse than that creepy character pawing her, having his way with her. *Think about something else.*

It did no good to think about what might happen, or about the filthy gag in her mouth and the tightness of the ropes on her ankles and wrists. So she turned her thoughts to other tight fixes from which she'd escaped during her past forays in exotic locales.

When she was fifteen, she'd visited the Hopi Indian reservation, where she stayed at a missionary's house. Reverend Tucker was a friend of her uncle, and he kept a close eye on her. But the only Hopis he knew were those who had been converted to Christianity, and their rituals weren't exotic enough to interest Diana or satisfy her curiosity, and she kept looking for an opportunity to talk to "real Hopis," as she thought of them.

Then one day she met a teenage boy, a few years older than she, who said he was the son of another missionary. He told her, in a conspiratorial tone, that if she met him that night outside the mission, he would take her to a Hopi elder who was teaching him about the kachinas.

She hesitated, but only a moment. She was leaving for home in the morning, and had just about given up hope of anything really exciting happening. But when she sneaked out, the boy was nowhere to be found.

She hung around for a while but quickly tired of waiting and decided he must have changed his mind. Then she heard drumming coming from the village and decided to take a look for herself.

She didn't realize, though, that a secret initiation ceremony, called the Astotokya, was taking place and that it was off-limits to everyone, except the participants. Even residents had to vacate the entire eastern half of the village.

She was caught by a guard before she'd entered the village and was taken to a small, windowless room. She was told that if she had crossed into the ceremonial area, all the initiates and priests would have been contaminated and none of them would have been allowed to live.

She apologized, but it didn't do any good. The penalty for her transgression was death. She would be dismembered, and bits of her flesh carried in the four directions by priests and buried before sunrise.

At first she thought they were just trying to frighten her, but then she recalled what the minister had said. One of the things he admired about the Hopis was that they didn't lie to him. Sometimes he didn't like what they said, but they were truthful. That was when she figured she really was in trouble.

The only thing that had saved her was the craftiness of the boy she was supposed to meet. He'd arrived late but in time to see her get caught by the guards. He'd dug a hole under the wall of the house where she was being held, and helped her escape.

She left for New York on schedule the next morning, grateful that she was still alive. But the odd thing was that when she'd asked Reverend Tucker about the boy on their way to the airport, he'd said there was no other missionary with a teenage son on the reservation.

She'd survived that incident, but how was she going to get out of this one? There'd been no talk of ransom, and now she was fairly certain that Xander Drax was behind her capture. He didn't need any money, but he might just want her dead.

She heard voices, then saw boots on the ladder as someone descended from the deck. She wiggled her arms and legs, trying to loosen the ties, but it was no use. Her skin was already burned raw.

Sala walked over to her, removed her gag. "So, how're we getting along, Diana?"

"*We* need some water."

Sala chuckled. "Yeah, I imagine you're a bit

thirsty by now.'' She held up a canteen. ''This what you're looking for?''

''Please,'' she whispered.

''Oh, I suppose.'' She held the canteen to Diana's lips; the water dribbled over her chin as she gulped. ''Is that better?'' She took a step back, crossed her arms, and studied Diana. ''You know, I can't figure out what's so important about you.''

''Then let me go.'' Diana's voice came back to her, and so did her feisty attitude. She disliked Quill, but Sala was the one who really annoyed her.

Sala laughed. ''I'm afraid not. I actually kind of like you.''

''Then let's get out of here.''

''So we can both be hunted? I don't think so.'' Sala paced back and forth and continued to scrutinize her. ''So tell me what's it like being so rich all the time. I'm real curious about that.''

''It's great. Look how much fun I'm having right now.'' Diana met Sala's burning gaze. ''What's *your* story, anyhow?''

''Nothing like yours. I grew up fast and never slowed down.'' She lowered her eyes. ''Nice boots. Expensive, I'll bet.''

''Not really.''

''C'mon. We can talk. It's just us girls.'' She bent down. ''Mind if I try on your boots?''

''Yeah, I mind.''

''Too bad.''

She tried to take off one of the boots, but Diana struggled to keep it on. She'd picked the boot containing the envelope.

''Cut it out!'' Sala said.

Sala pulled off the boot and the envelope fell to

the floor. Diana moved her feet over it before Sala saw it.

"I knew I was right," she said, glancing at the label inside the boot. "Fifth Avenue, New York City. My size, too. You don't need them right now. If Quill has his way, you won't ever be needing them again." She reached for the other boot—and saw the envelope. "What do we have here, Diana Palmer?"

Diana's stomach turned as Sala picked up the envelope, and read the name on the outside.

"Captain Philip Horton." She smiled at Diana. "A love letter, perhaps?"

She was about to open it when the laundry chute door flew open and a big purple thing flopped on a pile of towels and clothing. A man. He stood up. He was wearing tights and a jerkin with a belt, a hood and a mask.

He looked over at them. "What is this, a ship full of women?"

Diana was startled, but Sala seemed mesmerized. "All of my pilots are women."

"Interesting." The Phantom drew his knife, walked over to them, and casually pushed Sala aside. "Excuse me. I've got business with Ms. Palmer."

He moved over to Diana and cut the ropes binding her legs and arms.

"Who are you?" Diana asked as the ropes fell away. She couldn't take her eyes off him.

"A good Samaritan from the jungle."

"I'll bet you're better than good," Sala said. "You're the Phantom."

"That's a nickname. Ghost Who Walks is what they call me around here."

Whoever he was, Diana was grateful, as grateful

as she'd felt when the boy had rescued her that night on the Hopi reservation. But they weren't off this ship yet, she thought.

"Watch out!" Diana yelled as she leaped from the bench. But she was too late.

The Phantom turned just as Sala aimed a pistol at him. At the same moment, an alarm sounded throughout the ship. It distracted Sala long enough to give the Phantom the advantage. With lightning speed, he jerked the gun away from her. "Old jungle saying: 'Never point a gun at somebody. It might go off.'"

"Fast hands," Sala said. "I like that in a man. I really do."

She wrapped her arms around the Phantom's neck and gave him a long kiss on the mouth. When it was over, the Phantom showed no reaction. He pointed the gun at Sala and tossed Diana a length of rope.

"Tie her up."

Diana looked at the rope, then at Sala. She threw an uppercut that caught Sala under the jaw and nearly lifted her off her feet. She dropped to the floor, out cold.

"I see," the Phantom said.

"It's sort of personal," Diana said. "She wanted my boots."

"Let's go."

Diana retrieved her envelope and put on her boot. There was another thing that reminded her of the situation on the Hopi reservation. She hardly knew the boy who had saved her, and she had no idea who this Phantom was. "Not so fast. Why should I go with you?"

"Uh . . . yeah. Sure. You're Diana Palmer. Your

kidnapping's been reported to the authorities. This is a rescue.''

''Thanks. You've done a good job. I think I can handle it from here.''

Maybe Devil was really smart and that was why he led Zak into a narrow passageway between the deck and the cabins below. Or maybe the wolf was just doing what came natural, taking the most direct route he could find to reach Zak's father. Whatever the reason, the passageway kept wolf and boy out of sight of any crew members.

Zak just hoped that Devil knew where he was going. The space was so tight that he was concerned they wouldn't be able to turn around if they had to go back the same way they came in. Somehow they would have to get through the ceiling to his father, *if* Devil was able to find him.

Then Zak smelled food and noticed the tunnel was getting brighter. A few feet later, he came to a metal grating and could see down into a kitchen where three men were working. He sniffed again.

''Chicken soup,'' he said softly. His stomach growled in response.

He just hoped that Devil hadn't been lured here by the smell of food. But the wolf had only paused for a few seconds and was on the move again, through the tunnel.

They soon came to another grating and then another. Both looked down into a mess hall. More food smells. How could the wolf find his father's scent with all the distracting odors? Then Devil stopped. His tail swished and swatted Zak in the face.

''What is it?'' he whispered.

The wolf didn't move. He was staring intently down through another grating and growling softly. Zak could hear a voice and it sounded vaguely familiar. But it wasn't his father's voice.

He tapped Devil lightly on the back, hoping he'd move forward. "Good dog . . . I mean, good wolf," he whispered. Devil crawled forward, inching along on his stomach.

"I'll ask you one more time," the man said. "Will you do it?"

This time Zak recognized the voice. It was the man named Quill, the one with the skull tattooed on his face. The man who had nearly killed him. Quill moved to the side, and Zak saw that he was talking to someone tied to a chair.

"Papa!" he whispered.

Zak was relieved that he was still alive, but his sense of relief was immediately replaced with concern. How was he going to free him and get him off this freighter?

"I'm sorry, I can't lead you to his cave if I don't know where it is," his father said. His voice sounded hoarse. His head hung to one side. He looked even thinner than Zak remembered.

Quill's response was to kick the chair over and slam his fist against a table. Then he grabbed Zak's father by the hair and pulled him back up to a sitting position. "You're going to die if you don't talk. Is Ghost Who Walks worth more than your own life?"

No answer.

"You're a fool."

Quill pulled out a knife, then grabbed the native man by the hair again and jerked his head back. He pressed the knife to his throat and Zak screamed, "Noooo!"

Devil emitted a long, mournful howl.

But Quill never heard Zak or the wolf. Nor did he complete the act. An alarm blasted through the ship, blotting out all sounds. He stepped back, put his knife away, and pointed at Zak's father. "I'll get back to you. You're going to give me answers or you're dead."

As soon as Quill was out of the room, Zak pulled up the grating and shoved it aside. He hung by his hands from the ceiling and dropped to the floor. Then he rushed over to his father. "Papa, Papa!"

He hugged his father, who was so stunned by his sudden appearance that he didn't even react when a wolf dropped through the ceiling after him.

FIFTEEN

As Quill hurried down the corridor, several crew members scurried past him. Now what was it? Why couldn't he have any fun? Just as he was about to kill the native and then go enjoy himself with the rich girl, everything went haywire.

He wished now that he had snuffed Diana right away. It was what Xander Drax wanted, and Quill hadn't done it. Now if she got away, he was dead. He had been warned. Drax had no patience for anyone who didn't follow his orders.

He grabbed a crew member by the collar. "What the hell's going on?"

"There's a wild man in a purple suit and mask on the loose!"

"No! It can't be!" How could the Phantom have found him? Did he know about the girl? "Stop him! Scramble the pilots! Don't let him off this ship!"

"God, she hasn't changed a bit," the Phantom said to himself as he hurried after Diana.

He raced down a corridor, caught up to Diana, pulled her into a shadowy corner.

"Hey!" she snapped, trying to jerk free.

"Shhh."

He slapped his hand over her mouth as three crew members turned a corner and ran past them. "I think we should stick together."

"Okay," Diana conceded.

She started off again, but the Phantom pulled her back again. "I guess what I really meant was, we should stick together, but I should go first."

"Fine. After you. It's your rescue."

They headed off in the opposite direction of the three crew members and hurried down a corridor. The sound of boots against the metal floor brought them to a quick halt.

"In here!" the Phantom hissed, and opened a door. It was the crew quarters with the goggles and flight suits. "Hm, I've been here before."

Sure enough, the door to the adjoining locker room exploded open and the women pilots ran from the showers in their underwear. They stopped dead when they saw the Phantom and Diana.

The Phantom aimed his pistol at the women. "Ladies, where is your fashion sense? Flight suits are so déclassé. Don't you agree, Diana?"

"I certainly do," she said, and quickly gathered up the flight suits. Then, without a moment's hesitation, she pitched them out an open porthole.

"Good job," the Phantom said. "Shall we go?"

They slipped out of the crew quarters, raced down the corridor, then closed the big bulkhead door behind them. The Phantom turned the locking wheel and they scrambled up a ladder to the open deck.

"This way!" the Phantom hissed. "Fast!"

But as he ran around a corner, a man swung an iron bar at him. It struck his chest and he staggered backward, as several crew members pounced on him and Diana.

"I meant the other way," he muttered.

"Hold him!"

Quill, the man with the skull tattoo, the same one who had stolen the silver skull: The Phantom recognized him. But now he had matching skulls on his cheeks. The sight of the Sengh Brotherhood thug sent a surge of energy through the Phantom, and it took three crew members to keep him from charging right for Quill.

"Small world, huh? How's that knife wound healing?" Quill grinned. "Where was it again . . . right about here?" And he slammed the iron bar against the Phantom's side. Two more blows followed, each one hitting the spot where the knife had torn into him. "And I thought you'd fallen into the gorge. You're going to wish you had."

The Phantom doubled over in pain. Diana looked away.

Quill was about to strike him again when Devil flew out of his hiding place and leaped onto his back. Quill dropped to the deck, shrieking in surprise and pain as the snarling wolf mauled him.

"Good boy, Devil!" the Phantom yelled.

Despite the agony in his side, the Phantom threw off his two distracted attackers, and Devil turned on several others. His bloody muzzle and huge teeth were evidence enough that retreat was the wisest course. The thugs scattered like ants at a picnic, Devil snapping at their ankles.

The Phantom grabbed Diana. "Time to go."

"Your dog's a wolf." She said it with a mixture of awe and confusion.

"I know. Come on."

*　　*　　*

They dashed off across the deck. Behind them, Devil kept the other crew members occupied. Suddenly a man and a kid ran out and nearly collided with them.

"Zak! . . . and your father?"

"Ghost Who Walks," the man said in awe. "I am Yak, father of Zak."

"Good. No time to talk." The Phantom urged them forward and the four of them raced down the gangplank and along the dock.

The Phantom rushed over to one of the seaplanes. "Hurry! Get in!"

"Zak and I stay on the ground," Yak said, and loped off with his son.

The Phantom quickly untied the plane from its mooring. "Only room for two, anyhow."

Diana looked dubious. "You can fly a plane?" Then to herself, she added: "Of course you can. Why ask?"

They scrambled into the cockpit. The Phantom took the front seat and Diana the rear one. "Too bad I threw those flight suits away," she shouted to him as he revved the engine.

"We'll manage."

As the plane taxied away from the dock, the Phantom saw Quill limping down the gangplank, followed by a phalanx of his crew. "Stop them! Stop them! They're getting away!"

Several crew members raised pistols and fired. Bullets pinged against the fuselage, but the plane accelerated quickly, trailing two plumes of water. The Phantom pulled back on the yoke, pushed the throttle in, and the plane lifted smoothly from the waves.

He circled once above the cove and saw Quill and his men running to the foot of the dock where a truck was parked and a pair of saddled horses were hitched. In a matter of moments, the truck roared away in a cloud of dust with several men clinging to the running boards. Two men followed close behind on horseback.

Devil raced down the gangplank and ran down the dock, away from the ship. "Go!" the Phantom said as if Devil could hear him.

The wolf darted into the jungle to the spot where Hero patiently waited for the Phantom. Devil jumped up and down as if attempting to communicate with the stallion. Hero reared up on his hind legs, then galloped after Devil, who was already racing after the truck.

The fighter plane sped over the surf just a few hundred feet above the water. It felt good to be flying again, and in spite of their circumstances, the Phantom reveled in the sensation. He turned the plane toward the jungle, and pointed out Hero and Devil racing below the plane.

"They're fast!" Diana shouted over the din of the engine.

The Phantom glanced from the jungle floor to the instrument panel. To the fuel gauge. The arrow pointed to empty. "Oh, oh!"

"What is it?" Diana asked, leaning forward so he could hear her.

He craned his head and saw fuel spilling out from a bullet hole. "We're losing fuel. We've got to go down. No choice."

The Phantom feathered the engine; a plan started to form in his mind. The plane slowed and began to descend. It fell lower and lower until it clipped the top of several tall trees.

"What are you doing?" Diana yelled. "There's no place to land down there! This is a seaplane!"

Was this a rescue or just a different way to die? Diana almost wished she was back on the freighter.

"Climb down onto the pontoons."

"What?" He didn't say that.

"Climb down onto the pontoons."

"Why?"

"Like you said . . . there's no place to land down there," the Phantom answered.

"Then what?"

"Trust me."

Trust him. Sure. "One of us is crazy," she muttered.

She climbed from the cockpit onto the wing. Using the struts and support wire to keep her balance, she slid down onto the pontoon. Good thing she did well in gymnastics. Somebody less nimble wouldn't have made it. She clutched the pontoon, the wind biting her eyes until they teared.

A clearing opened like an eye in the jungle, a pale slit in all the green.

The Phantom brought the plane in even lower. They were only ten or twelve feet from the ground when he swung down from the wing and joined Diana on the pontoon.

"Who, uh, is flying the plane?"

"I jammed the throttle."

"You jammed . . . oh great, that's just great."

"We don't have much time. This clearing isn't very long."

"Count me out."

"Too late for that."

"I think—"

"Get ready!" the Phantom snapped.

"Get ready?" For what? Her unspoken question was answered when a white stallion appeared beneath the plane, galloping in perfect rhythm, keeping pace with the descending plane.

"No way," she said, shaking her head, trying to laugh. "You can't be—"

"We have to. Meet Hero; he's a good horse."

With that, the Phantom lowered himself from the pontoon and dangled several feet off the ground until the stallion was directly below him.

Then he let go and landed in the saddle. The Phantom dropped his head back, looking up at her, and extended his arms. "Jump! Now!"

And she did.

She landed in the Phantom's arms.

Hero never even broke stride. The jungle now loomed in front of them, a wall of green. Surely they'd be clobbered by a limb or shredded by branches. But the Phantom grabbed the reins and veered off.

She looked up to see the plane continue on, moving in a collision course with a stand of gumbo limbo trees. A moment later, the plane vanished into the trees and exploded. A huge orange fireball leaped into the sky.

The impact from the blast rolled over them in hot, rippling waves. Then they thundered through it, past it, following the edge of the clearing.

Diana squeezed her eyes shut and surrendered herself to sensation: the hard reality of the saddle beneath her; the strength of the Phantom's arm encircling her waist; the speed with which Hero moved; the wind against her face.

These things were real.

She opened her eyes, the green rushed toward her, Devil raced along beside them, loping with the grace of the stallion, keeping pace with them.

"Did we really do that? I can't believe we just did that!"

"Neither can I," the Phantom said.

"Where are we going?"

"Away from trouble."

But it wasn't quite that simple. Trouble was just ahead, lying in wait like some ravenous predator.

SIXTEEN

The truck raced off the road and slammed through the underbrush. With every rut, every pothole, the bites Quill had sustained from the Phantom's bloody wolf burned and ached. Suppose the damn animal was rabid? Suppose the bites got infected? That bastard the Phantom would pay for this, he thought.

They bounced over a hill and into a clearing. Quill knew the gas tank on the plane had been hit at least once and wouldn't fly far. It had to be in here somewhere. There had to be some sign of it. "Where'd it go? I just saw it," he muttered.

The answer came with a booming explosion that set the jungle on fire. Quill let out a triumphant whoop. "Well, I guess that takes care of that little problem. Time to go home, boys. Mission complete. Two dead and one silver skull for the boss."

"Look!" the driver shouted, and pointed across the grassy opening.

Quill did a quick double-take. He could hardly believe what he saw. The purple bastard and the woman should be dead in the crash, but instead they were riding in tandem on the big white stallion like circus performers. And that unearthly wolf-dog, whatever it was, was chasing along behind them.

"After them. Move it!"

He pounded the dashboard, wishing he were behind the wheel, but he was in no shape to drive. His right side—his leg, buttock, and lower back—burned with bite wounds.

The blood was starting to dry and cake on his skin. His shirt and pants were sticking to his wounds. He would attend to that later. He could handle the pain for now. Until those two were dead—really dead—nothing else mattered.

Quill was dangerous when his anger and frustration boiled over, and the sight of the pair on horseback sent him well over the top. His anger made him crazy, and it always got him in trouble. Not that he really thought about it that way. But deep inside, he knew it was true. He never really wanted to be a professional crook, the bad guy, but he'd just dug himself deeper and deeper until that was what he was. He didn't know anything else. He could kill without a second thought, and he was ready to kill now.

"Faster!" he shouted, and smashed his fist against the driver's shoulder as if he were spurring on a horse.

The men on the running board were firing round after round and missing every time. Quill pulled out his pistol. He would take them both out himself. He would just wound the wolf, though, and let it die slowly and painfully. Then he'd take the stallion as his personal trophy. Before he left for the States, he would see if the stallion would lead him home—to the Phantom's home and all of its treasures.

He threw open the passenger door so hard it knocked one of his men off the running board. He dropped into the man's place, and took aim at the thePhantom and Diana. He fired and missed, fired again and missed again. The truck was bouncing too damn much.

Cursing through his gritted teeth, he turned his aim on the wolf, but before he squeezed off a round, the beast suddenly dashed into the jungle. The gunfire spooked the wolf, Quill thought, that was the reasonable explanation. But he couldn't shake the certainty that the wolf had heard his thoughts.

The Phantom pulled up hard on the reins and the stallion came to a quick stop, then pranced in a tight circle. He was looking around. Ah, the wolf—he probably thought it had been shot, Quill figured.

Quill smacked the window with his fist and motioned the driver to hit the brakes. He aimed at the purple target, bracing his arm with his other hand as the truck skidded to a dead stop. "Nobody shoot. He's mine!"

Got 'im now. He fired.

But just as he pulled the trigger, someone knocked his arm and the shot flew wide. He spun around and grabbed the man behind him by his collar.

"I didn't do anything!" He raised his hands in protest and shook his head.

Quill didn't want to hear it. He put the gun to the man's face and pulled the trigger. Click!

Out of bullets. He let go and the wide-eyed man, shrinking in fear, toppled backward off the running board.

Quill spun around just as the Phantom and Diana charged into the jungle, leaning low over the stallion.

He ducked back into the cab and pulled bullets from his gun belt to reload the pistol.

"Go! Go! After them," he shouted. "What in blazes are you waiting for, a formal invite?"

"But there's no road that way!" the driver pleaded.

"Then make one!"

The truck plowed into the woods after the stallion. The horse darted through a thick grove of trees, and the riders alternately looked up and ducked as limbs barely missed knocking them to the ground.

Quill was so transfixed by the scene that he was only vaguely aware that the men on the running board had either jumped or been knocked off by the branches swatting the sides of the truck. It was just him and the driver.

"Go down! Go down!" Quill muttered, anticipating the moment when the Phantom and the girl would be slammed to the ground.

"Go down where?" the driver asked, misunderstanding Quill.

"Shut up and drive!"

The stink of smoke seeped through the dense forest. The stallion suddenly reared up as flames from the fire engulfed a nearby tree. The horse was clearly afraid and unwilling to go further.

The truck surged ahead. "Got ya now!" A maniacal grin spread across Quill's face.

Then, suddenly, a loud screech ripped through the cab. Branches pounded the windshield, the truck slammed into two trees and wedged between them. Quill was thrown forward and his injured right leg cracked hard against the underside of the dashboard. He rolled onto the floor, grabbing the leg.

"Ahhh!" he yelled out in pain. "Can't you drive!"

He looked out to see the stallion with its riders charging away to his left, on a new path away from the fire. Two of his men on horseback pulled up alongside the truck. Livid with pain and rage, Quill shouted at them to catch the riders.

"Don't let them get away!"

"The horses are afraid of the smoke," one of the riders yelled.

"So is *his* horse. Go after him. Now!"

As they galloped after the Phantom, Quill realized his other foot was wedged in the springs underneath the seat. He pulled and twisted, but couldn't free his foot. He glanced out the door and nearly swallowed his tongue. A wall of flames danced toward him. In moments he could feel the heat, hear the crackling of the flames as they consumed everything in their path.

"My foot. I can't get out. Someone help me!"

The driver leaped out and loped away from the truck and the fire.

"Hey, get back here!" Quill screamed.

The man kept on running.

Moments after the truck crashed into the trees, Zak pulled off the tarp that had covered him and his father during the wild ride.

"I smell smoke," Yak whispered.

"Me too."

When they'd climbed into the truck, they'd had no idea that Quill and his men were about to join them. Fortunately the men had ridden in the cab and on the running board, so they'd gone undetected. Zak had found a hole in the truck's canvas wall, and he'd seen enough to know that the Phantom and Diana had somehow survived the crash and were riding away on Hero. He'd also seen Quill taking aim. That was when he'd stuck his hand through the hole and shoved Quill's arm just as he'd fired at the Phantom.

They scrambled out of the back of the truck just as the driver abandoned the vehicle and fled into the jungle. Flames shot toward the sky. In no time, the truck and everything around it would be engulfed.

Then they heard someone yelling inside the cab of the truck. "Someone needs help," Yak said.

"It's the bad one," Zak said.

"It doesn't matter."

Zak moved around the side of the truck. He could feel the heat from the fire now. Quill was on his back on the floor, clutching his injured leg, his other foot jammed under the seat. He was trapped there like a bird in a cage.

Quill looked startled to see Yak and Zak but recovered quickly. He aimed his pistol at Yak. "Get me out of here or I'll shoot."

"If you shoot us, you won't get out," Yak said calmly. "Put the gun down. The fire is coming very quickly."

Quill's face twisted in anger and pain. Then he lowered the gun and dropped it. Yak picked it up and hurled it into the jungle. He leaned over and worked Quill's foot free. Zak helped pull him out of the truck.

Quill stood up, hobbled on one leg, then leaned against the truck. Flames were already flickering in the underbrush. "What are you going to do, eat me after I'm cooked?"

Yak looked around, then pointed in the direction

the truck had come from. "Go that way. You can get away from the fire."

Quill looked warily at Yak, then limped away.

"Why, Papa? Why did you let him go?"

"It would be good to let him roast in the truck, I know. But sometimes we must make sacrifices for the greater good. Do you understand?"

Zak shook his head.

Yak smiled. "You will soon enough."

Father and son dashed into the forest. They weren't far from their village, at least not far using their traditional method of transportation. "Do you think the fire will burn our village, Papa?"

Yak pointed to the sky where dark rain clouds had formed. "The spirits are already working for us. They accepted our sacrifice. The village and the forest will be saved."

Drops of rain struck his head as if in confirmation. Then Yak grabbed a long, thick vine that hung from one of the trees, swung up into the branches, grabbed another vine, and swung it toward his son.

Zak caught it, laughed, and quickly followed his father into the deep forest.

SEVENTEEN

Hero dashed through the forest, picking a path that avoided heavy underbrush and low branches. The Phantom could tell that the stallion was at ease now that they were clear of the fire and smoke. He galloped with a smooth, relaxed rhythm. With two riders on his back, his pace was slower, but he didn't seem to be wearing down.

The Phantom hadn't expected the fire since the fuel had been so low. But apparently there had been enough to set off the explosion. He hoped the rain, which was starting to fall, would control the fire before it spread.

"We lost them," Diana said finally.

The Phantom glanced back. "Not yet."

Two men on horseback were gaining on them. "We can't outrun them doubled up like this," she said. "Do you have any ideas?"

"Yeah, don't worry. I've got plenty of friends in this forest."

The Phantom pointed upward at a vast network of ropes, vines, and nets hanging from the trees. Here and there, faces were visible, watching them as they sped past, deeper and deeper into the dense forest.

When the Phantom looked back again, the two riders had closed the gap. They drew their pistols and took aim. One fired, then the other. The Phantom and Diana ducked to avoid a thick limb just as a bullet struck it; chips of wood spattered onto their heads. Another bullet missed the Phantom's shoulder by inches.

The Phantom was starting to get worried now, but before the riders could fire again, they were abruptly yanked from their saddles by ropes with nooses that had been dropped from above. The men were jerked straight upward, crashing through the limbs and branches. Yelling and cursing, they vanished into the thick forest canopy.

Several Rope People, acting as counterweights, came down as the riders went up. The Phantom reined in Hero; Diana stared up in amazement. "How did they do that, anyway?" she asked.

"It's all done with hooks, pulleys, and winches. They've got a lot of practice."

"Look!" She pointed at the Rope People who dropped to the ground.

Zak and Yak waved and ran over to them. Rain was pouring down now, but the high forest canopy acted as an umbrella, and it seeped through only as a soft, fine spray.

"My friends, the Rope People."

"How did you get here so fast?" Diana asked, astonished to see Zak and his father.

Yak just pointed to the trees.

"Never underestimate the speed of travel by rope," the Phantom said. "But you've got to grow up with it."

"I'd like to hear more about it. I never knew about

the Rope People. The Bangallans are even more interesting than I'd imagined.''

''Can you stay with us for a while?'' Yak asked. ''I want to thank you for saving my son's life.''

''I'd love to,'' Diana replied before the Phantom could get in a word. ''I'd like to hear all your stories.''

Zak laughed. ''That would take years.''

''Maybe some other time,'' the Phantom said. ''We have to be moving right along.''

Diana looked disappointed. ''I'll make a point of coming back.''

Several more Rope People dropped like blossoms from the trees. She immediately began talking with them, and the Phantom went over to Yak. ''You can be very proud of your son. He's a brave kid. He's the one who saved you.''

''With the help of your wolf,'' Zak said. ''Where's Devil?''

As soon as he asked the question, the wolf leaped from the nearby foliage. Most of the Rope People shrank back in surprise and fear, chattering among themselves and pointing. Then they laughed when the wolf trotted over to Zak and licked his face.

''Good, boy. Good, boy,'' Zak said, hugging him. ''I wish I had a wolf just like you.''

The Phantom turned to Diana. ''We need to be on our way, pronto.''

It all seemed like a dream to Diana. Everything was happening so fast. The masked man's rescue and the escape from the freighter. Flying and crashing a plane and landing on a white stallion. Fleeing in the jungle and meeting the Rope People. And now she was racing deep into the forest with the purple-garbed masked man.

She drank in the sights and sounds around her. The forest was lush and green, and every sort of plant and animal imaginable blurred past them. The songs of birds, the buzz of insects, the calls of monkeys and leopards and a thousand others filled her head. She felt dizzy, unable to imagine what could be in store for her next. She didn't even want to think about it.

"Are you okay?" the Phantom asked, leaning forward, his breath warm against her hair, her ear. His arms tightened around her and she welcomed it.

"I feel a little light-headed. I guess I haven't had much sleep lately."

"And the humidity can make you drowsy."

The rain had stopped, the water now rising as steam from the floor of the forest, and the afternoon was quickly turning to dusk. As the jungle's sounds and shadows became disembodied from their origins in the failing light, the jungle became even more mysterious.

It was as if Diana had stumbled into a mythological world where the magnificent and the grotesque coexisted. At any moment tigers might leap out at them, a boa constrictor might drop from the trees, the sun might burst through the forest. Flesh-eating plants might trip Hero, wrap themselves around the horse and riders, and feed on them until they were nothing more than skeletons.

Her imagination went wild. The stallion waded across a shallow stream, and Diana was sure she saw a dozen pairs of red crocodile eyes moving across the surface of the water toward them. "Look!" She pointed toward the dark waters as a crocodile raised its head out of the water.

"They're just curious. As long as we don't stop, we're okay," the Phantom assured her. "Of course, you don't want to fall in, either." Then he held her closer and spurred Hero, who bolted forward, out of the water and onto a trail that he alone could see.

There was something oddly familiar about the Phantom. It seemed ridiculous, yet she couldn't get over the sensation. She was certain that she would've remembered a character in purple tights and a mask.

Had she met him, perhaps, when he was in regular clothes? Certainly from the way he spoke, it was obvious that he spent a good deal of time away from the jungle. He was no wild man.

They rode for a long time, and when twilight finally overtook them, the Phantom slowed Hero to a trot. Diana noticed the sound of running water growing louder and louder, until it was a thunderous roar.

A waterfall appeared then, glimmering in the moonlight. They were thirty feet below the top and another thirty feet above the swirling pool that caught the falls.

At first Diana thought that he had brought her here just to see the awesome power of the falls and enjoy the stupendous sight. But he nudged Hero, who trotted confidently forward toward the falls, then through the sparkling curtain of water. She was covered in a fine, cool spray that was the most refreshing shower she'd ever had after a long trip.

But the journey wasn't over yet. In a sense it was just beginning. Hero carried them across the dry cavern behind the falls and out the other side. They paused a moment, gazing over the landscape.

A pristine valley opened up in the moonlight below them. It probably hadn't changed in a thousand or ten thousand years. Even at night, it was easy to see that the forest was older and less dense than anything they had traversed.

Somehow she knew it was friendlier, too. She had no fear of being attacked by vicious creatures. It was the sort of place where she had always wanted to have a home, a place to escape from the hectic pace of big city life, which she realized she enjoyed less and less each time she returned home.

"It's beautiful, just beautiful. Breathtaking," she said.

"Magical, I think that's the word. It's called Deep Woods. Wait until you see it in the daylight. There's no place quite like it."

"Does that mean we're not going to just pass on through it?"

The Phantom didn't answer. Instead he spurred Hero, and they rode swiftly across the valley floor. Hero seemed to gallop with an unbridled joy now, knowing he had arrived home. Yes, she was sure they were very near the Phantom's secret home, and she wondered what sort of place it would be.

A cliff rose above the forest, and protruding from it was a huge rock formation at least eighty feet high. It had been carved by the wind and rain into the shape of a skull. Two large caves formed the eyesockets of the skull. An avalanche or maybe a millennium of weathering had left a gash that looked amazingly like the ruins of a nose. An enormous cavern at least thirty feet across and fifteen feet high formed the mouth.

A skull cave, she thought, and she knew this was

where the Phantom lived. She tried not to form any preconceptions of what it must be like inside, but her mind had already painted a dim, gloomy picture. Mold, darkness, snakes, God knew what else. The Waldorf it wasn't.

Then the day's events caught up with her, overwhelmed her. She was suddenly so tired she couldn't keep her eyes open and nodded off. Now and then she surfaced from wherever she'd gone and was aware that as Hero pranced through the opening of the cave, the Phantom murmured, "Home, sweet home," and that she laughed softly and drifted away again.

She was asleep when Hero finally stopped. The Phantom carried Diana into Skull Cave and set her down on a pile of woven mats.

Guran immediately appeared and covered her with blankets. The Phantom adjusted the blankets, then gently brushed her light-brown hair away from her face.

"Who is she?" Guran asked, his voice soft.

"Her name is Diana Palmer." A beat passed as he gazed thoughtfully at her. "I know her, Guran. From before. From America . . ."

Guran watched in silence as the Phantom got to his feet and walked outside the cave. He sat down on a rock and looked out over the dark valley, which was blanketed with a silver glaze of moonlight.

The first time he met her was when she was staying on the Hopi Indian Reservation. He was seventeen and traveling the world with his father, who was showing him all the hideouts. They were staying in one of those hideouts, a spot located at the top of a high, sheer mesa.

The Hopis and other Pueblo Indians knew it as Walker's Table, a place thought to be haunted by spirits, among them the Ghost Who Walks. Kit had been fascinated by the Hopi's kachinas, which were a lot like the nature spirits and spirit guides of the Bangallan tribes. He was intrigued by how cultures, separated by thousands of miles, had such similar beliefs in an invisible world that was intricately connected with the forces of nature.

When he'd met Diana, he'd told her he was staying with another missionary in one of the other Hopi villages. He was amazed by how readily she'd accepted his offer to sneak out and visit an old Hopi storyteller. On the night they were to meet, he was going to take her to an old man who had recognized him as a young initiate of a powerful tradition. He'd been teaching Kit about the powers of the kachinas, and he'd agreed to allow Diana to join him.

But Kit had arrived late, and instead of waiting for him, Diana had wandered into big trouble when she nearly walked into a secret initiation ceremony. He'd put to use all of the skills his father had taught him to save her, and he was still lucky he'd succeeded.

He'd met her again three years later when he was a senior at Columbia University and she was a sophomore. They saw each other regularly for eight months until he graduated. She never connected him with the boy from the reservation who'd saved her, and he'd never told her. But then, he'd never told her a lot of things about himself.

Maybe it was time she knew.

EIGHTEEN

The sun cut through the mist that rose from the valley floor. The light shimmered, creating magical illusions of etheric dancing beings that skipped from treetop to treetop, rock to rock. Diana looked out in amazement over the valley.

"So, it wasn't a dream," she murmured.

But of all the incredible things she had seen, the Phantom took the prize. Who was he? *What* was he? And where was he? For that matter, where was she in relation to anything else? Where was New York from here?

She stood up from her bed inside the mouth of the cave. "Hello," she called. "Anybody here?"

She saw eyes and ears, a snout. Devil was crouched near the other wall, watching her intently. No one here but the wolf, she thought. "Devil, where's your master? Did he go someplace?"

The wolf merely stared at her. It looked neither friendly nor angry. Just watchful.

She moved farther into the cave, exploring it, and realized it penetrated deep into the cliff. "What kind of man lives in a cave?"

The first thing she saw was a huge, high-backed

chair on a raised platform. It was adorned with skulls. "Papa Bear's chair," she said, glancing at Devil. "I have to tell you I'm not real crazy about the motif. Is this where your master sits?"

Devil, who had followed her at a distance, now sat down and cocked his head. He whined and pawed the ground.

"I take it that means yes."

Another whine. He pawed the ground again.

She decided to try the chair and sat down in it, careful not to touch the skulls embedded in the arms. Devil growled; his flaring eyes burned into her.

"Oh, c'mon, Devil. I'm just trying it out. No big deal, okay?"

Devil answered with another low, grumbling growl. Her amusement at the wolf's reaction shifted to concern. "Hey, I'm not hurting anything, boy."

The hairs on the back of the wolf's neck rose. His growling deepened and grew more threatening.

"Okay, okay. I get the idea. I'm getting off."

She got up slowly, her eyes glued to the wolf, wary that he might attack. But as soon as she moved away from the throne, the wolf relaxed. Devil still regarded her with suspicion, as though he expected her to try out the throne again, but he no longer seemed intent on assaulting her. There were obviously some very clear-cut rules here in the cave.

She turned her palms up. "Where is he, anyway?

The wolf just stared back at her.

"Fine. I'll find him myself."

Devil whined, pawed again at the ground, and trotted after her as she walked out of the cave.

Diana followed a well-traveled path into the forest. A hundred bright red, yellow, and cobalt butterflies flickered along the trail from one orange and purple tubular flower to another. The trail led to a quiet lagoon shrouded by flowering bushes. Green parrots flitted from branch to branch in the treetops, and a family of squirrel monkeys swung through the trees, arguing noisily.

Diana noticed the Phantom's purple outfit draped across a rock. She crept closer and ducked behind a bush. A man was bathing in the river, his back turned toward her so she couldn't see his face.

But she liked what she saw. A firm, lean body, muscular thighs, broad muscular shoulders.

She heard a growl behind her and her head snapped around. Devil crouched low. This time the wolf's growl was deep and ominous.

"Not you again," she said softly. "Who are you—his mother? He brought me here, you know. That makes me a guest. You should probably be a little nicer."

She glanced back at the lagoon and wondered if the Phantom had heard her voice or Devil's growls. His clothes were no longer on the rock. She started to stand up, but Devil grabbed her by the sleeve of her blouse. Then the wolf pulled her away.

"Hey! What are you doing?"

She tried to jerk her arm free, but Devil kept tugging on her sleeve. No matter what she did, she couldn't get him to release it.

"Devil! Release!"

The wolf instantly let go of her arm. The Phantom, now astride Hero, towered over them. To her disappointment, he was back in costume, complete with mask.

"Sorry. Wolves are a bit territorial," the Phantom told her.

"Who *are* you?"

"We've already been through that."

"That's not what I mean. Don't you have a real name?"

"Not anymore."

"Then what *was* your real name?"

"I forget."

She rolled her eyes. "Right."

"Any more questions?"

Diana laughed. "Just a million of them."

"They'll have to wait. Captain Horton is on his way to meet you."

A throng of butterflies fluttered around them, and several landed on the Phantom's arms and shoulders. One rested on Devil's snout. Then, moving en masse, they fluttered upward and circled the lagoon.

The Phantom extended his hand. "C'mon, we'll take the scenic route. I think you'll like it." He pulled her up into the saddle with him.

"This feels all too familiar," she commented. "You know, I'm not completely recovered yet from yesterday."

"It wasn't *that* bad."

"Ha."

"We'll take it easy."

They rode through the dappled shadows of a lush jungle path. Diana felt as if she were touring a giant open-air botanical garden and arboretum. But someone had forgotten to mark the names on all the plants. She recognized the elephant-ear philodendra, which were house plants in New York but grew in a riotous profusion here.

They continued on up a hillside with a commanding view of the secret valley. The sight of it literally took her breath away. Light greens melted into emerald greens. Reds and violets, vivid yellows and golds burned in all the green. Here and there were soft blues and aquas. An artist's palette.

But in spite of the beauty and grandeur of this place, Diana sensed that the Phantom was lonely. As far as she knew, he and his animals lived alone here.

The Phantom kept his arm around her waist as they rode. She felt the warmth and pressure of his skin and decided she liked it. His closeness was gentle, yet firm.

"You called this place the Deep Woods yesterday," she said.

"That's right."

"Your domain?"

"It's where I live."

"So you're some kind of jungle lord and this is your kingdom. Very nice. And you go out and save women in distress from time to time for variety."

"Beats punching a time clock."

She laughed. "I suppose. But doesn't it get lonely here for a young man?"

He shrugged and didn't answer right away. It was as if he'd never considered the question before. "I have Guran here, and the animals, of course. But—"

"Guran?" Was he living with a native woman? She suddenly felt jealous and was instantly appalled at her reaction. How could she feel jealous? She'd just met the man. Didn't even know his real name. Had never see his face. Ridiculous.

"You'll meet him soon enough. He's on his way with Captain Horton."

"Oh, I see," she said, relieved to know that Guran was a man.

"But before they arrive, I want to show you one of my favorite places."

They galloped off through the forest on another trail. Before long, a warm salty breeze filled the air. Water glittered between the trees; she heard the roar of a surf. The forest gave way to a beautiful, pristine beach, and beyond it was the ocean.

They galloped half a mile along the beach and through the surf, and finally came to a halt. The Phantom dismounted, then helped Diana down from Hero.

She stretched out her arms and swung about in a circle. "This is incredible."

"It's Keela Wee Beach."

"It's like Paradise."

"It *is* Paradise."

Hero wasn't very impressed. The horse walked away from the water and stood in the shade of an enormous banyan tree. Its branches spread out in every direction.

She scooped up a handful of sand and let it sift through her fingers. The light danced against it. "What makes it sparkle like that?"

"Gold."

"You're kidding."

"I never kid."

The Phantom had picked up a coconut that had fallen from one of the tall palms. He pulled a machete from the saddlebag and chopped off the top of an enormous coconut. He handed it to her. "You want a drink?"

"Well, I am thirsty. Oh . . . it's heavy." She lifted

it unsteadily to her mouth, tasted the coconut milk, then drank deeply. She passed it back to the Phantom.

Devil loped toward them along the beach with something in his mouth. "Look, what's he got?"

"I sent him out for bananas."

Diana burst out laughing and shook her head. "You're filled with surprises."

The wolf sat down in front of the Phantom and dropped the clump of bananas. "Good boy," the Phantom said. "Thanks."

"This is amazing," Diana said as she ate one of the bananas. "Drinks and fruit and . . ."

". . . And plenty of lobsters and fish," the Phantom added, sweeping a hand toward the sea.

"And gold," she said, digging her bare feet into the sand. "Don't people come here and try to steal the gold?"

"People don't come here *at all* without my permission," he replied.

They walked along the beach toward the jungle. "I can certainly see why you love it here."

"Did I say that?"

"You don't have to."

"I guess I'm just an open book," the Phantom said with a laugh.

"Not as long as you're hiding behind that mask," Diana responded.

"Hide? In this getup?"

"Then take off your mask."

"I'd rather not."

His face was probably disfigured or something, she thought, and immediately spun a dozen different stories about how it had happened. A fight, a fire, or perhaps he was born with the disfigurement.

Something in the underbrush at the edge of the jungle caught her attention. Movement. And whatever it was looked large. Very large.

"What is it?" the Phantom asked.

"Ah . . . behind you. I don't know what . . ."

Then it stepped out into full view. A lion. Its body tensed and muscles rippled; it crouched low as though it were ready to spring. Diana froze where she was, afraid to twitch, afraid to breathe. The ocean, she thought. They could race into the surf and wait for the lion to go away.

But before she moved, the lion darted forward and leaped onto the Phantom, knocking him to the ground. Diana screamed and jumped back as the Phantom struggled with the beast. Locked together, they rolled over and over, kicking up a cloud of sand. The Phantom groaned and grunted; the lion growled and roared.

Horrified, Diana's feet uprooted from the sand, she grabbed a coconut, and charged forward. Then she realized the Phantom was laughing. The lion was licking his ear and the Phantom was scratching its belly.

Diana angrily threw down the coconut. "You're playing!" She shook her head in amazement. "You're playing with a lion."

"This guy's an old friend," he said, getting to his feet. "Here. Scratch him. It's good for the soul, Diana."

She knelt down tentatively next to the lion and began to scratch its belly. Even though the beast was the Phantom's friend, she was still wary. One playful swat from the creature's paw might send her directly into the great beyond.

"Go on. Don't be afraid," the Phantom said encouragingly. Dig your fingers in deep. He likes it."

The lion stretched and purred contentedly as she worked her fingers into its pelt.

"That's better," the Phantom said. "You're getting the hang of it." A few yards away, Hero was stomping the ground and shaking his head. The Phantom walked over to him. "What, you're jealous of that big old lion, Hero? That's not like you."

Diana walked over to him. "When I left New York, I certainly didn't think that I'd be playing with a lion in paradise."

"You haven't met the whole crew yet."

As soon as he said it, a python slithered down from the branches and wrapped its body around the Phantom's throat, like some huge, grotesque necklace.

She tried to remain unconcerned as the Phantom struggled with the massive creature. "Let's see, a wolf, a lion, and now a python. Strange bunch of friends."

The Phantom pried the python off his neck and, gasping for air, threw it into the underbrush. He took a deep breath and rubbed his throat. "I never met that snake before in my life."

NINETEEN

"**W**e better get going. Horton should be arriving any time." After his encounter with the python, the Phantom was ready to leave.

He stroked Hero's neck as he mounted him. "Next time I'll pay closer attention to you."

He helped Diana up into the saddle in front of him. "Hero was trying to tell us about the snake, but I walked right into the serpent's little trap."

"Does that happen often?" she asked as they galloped away.

"If it did, I wouldn't be around to tell you about it. Life in the jungle, you know."

"Yeah, I know. I live in New York, remember?" Diana said. "It can be like a jungle, too. It's not like it used to be. It's quite dangerous now, you know. The Depression has made a lot of people quite desperate."

"I suppose," the Phantom said vaguely.

He remembered New York with Diana. Everything had been magical in their time together. It was almost as if they had been floating through life while it lasted, but it had ended too soon and abruptly. A lot had been left unsaid, and he had regretted it.

When they arrived at Skull Cave and dismounted, the Phantom turned to Diana. ''Wait here a moment.'' He had a surprise for her.

He hurried into the cave and ducked around the Skull Throne. Then he slipped into a narrow passageway that led into the Treasure Room.

The room was piled high with gold and silver objects, many embedded with gems. There were intricate carvings in jade and lapis, and treasures of jewelry, diamonds, and gold coins. Some of the objects were ancient and priceless.

There was no way of estimating their value. They all had been accumulated over the centuries for services rendered. Each one had a story that went with it, and his father had told him many of them. But for every object with a story, there was another with a past that had long been forgotten.

The Phantom glanced around, found what he was looking for, and snatched it up. He hurried out to the entrance of the cave. Diana was standing near the rim, looking intently out over the valley. He caught his breath as he walked up to her.

''Two people on horseback just entered the valley,'' Diana said. ''I saw Devil with them.''

The Phantom knew it was Horton and Guran. Devil would have alerted him with a howl if it had been strangers, who virtually never found their way into the valley, unless he led them here.

''I just want to give you something to remember me by,'' he said, glad they were still alone.

''Somehow I don't think remembering you is going to be a problem,'' she replied with a smile.

He held out a necklace. ''You won't find these in New York.''

Diana cupped the necklace in her palms. "Black pearls. They're beautiful. But I don't think I can accept them. I mean, I should be giving you something."

He smiled. "You already have. Please, take them. I insist."

She was quiet a moment. He ran her fingers over the pearls, then looked up at him. "Okay. If you insist. Is there a story that comes with them?"

"They were given to one of my ancestors by a grateful Arabian prince after my great-great grandfather rescued the young woman he was going to marry from an enemy."

"Ah, another rescue story. I guess it's an appropriate gift then."

Her eyes suddenly glistened with tears. "Thank you, Phantom. I'm touched."

"Oh, no—not the old pearl ploy again!"

The Phantom and Diana both turned to see Horton and Guran stepping into the cave. "That's what passes for humor in the jungle, Diana," the Phantom said apologetically. "Say hello to Captain Horton and Guran."

"Thank God you're all right, Diana. We were monitoring the situation on our radio from the time the plane went down." He turned to the Phantom. "So how did you manage to get her away?"

"Diana did most of the work. All I did was clear the path."

"He's not just mysterious, he's modest, too," Diana said.

Horton took out his pipe. "Old jungle saying: 'The Phantom is many men.' "

The Phantom noticed that Horton was about to

light his pipe, and nudged Guran, who spoke up. "No smoking in Skull Cave."

"Oh. Sorry. I forgot." He shook out the match. "I received your uncle's wire, Diana. What could be so important to bring you all this way?"

She reached into the pocket of her slacks and took out the envelope she'd been carrying since she left New York. "Can you identify this symbol?" she asked, removing the piece of paper.

Horton looked at the spider-web design and made a sour face. He showed the Phantom the symbol. "Interesting."

"Will somebody say something? What does it mean?" Diana asked, exasperated.

The Phantom handed her the slip of paper. "It means you're mixed up with the Sengh Brotherhood."

"The what?"

"The Sengh Brotherhood. An ancient order of evil," Horton explained. "They started out as pirates. Nowadays, there's no telling what they've become."

"Where did you get this, Diana?" the Phantom asked.

He was intensely curious about it. He knew that Quill was associated with the Brotherhood, but he'd had no idea why he was interested in Diana.

"New York. My uncle's newspaper is investigating a man named Xander Drax. He's crazy. He's wealthy, manipulative, and greedy. He's a power-mad financier and industrialist who uses coercion whenever he can to gain what he wants. He's dangerous, and he wants to possess a supernatural force that originated in this jungle."

The Phantom knew, of course, exactly what

Xander Drax wanted: the Skulls of Touganda. But he wasn't aware that the Sengh Brotherhood had extended its influence into the United States. He wondered if this Drax had managed to gain power, if not control, of the Brotherhood. Drax sounded like an industrial pirate, and they were every bit as bad as the traditional sort.

He had to be careful what he said to Diana. He didn't want to get her any more involved. She didn't need to know about the skulls. As it was now, her life was in danger. "The Bangalla jungle is full of strange and dangerous things, Diana."

He looked over to Horton. "Captain, I want you to take Diana back. Use every man at your disposal. Give her all the protection she needs."

"Certainly."

"What? That's it? You're sending me away?" Diana fixed her hands to her hips, miffed at his cavalier dismissal. "I'm not done here yet. I need to know more. Much more! Don't you understand? This is urgent. What is Drax after? I want to know."

"All you need to know is that you've helped me in ways that I can never explain."

"Oh, puh-lease," she muttered. "Enough of the Mr. Mysterious stuff, okay?"

"I've said all I've got to say," the Phantom replied. "Bye, Diana. Take care." Then he walked back into the cave.

"Well, I can tell when I'm not welcome," Diana said as she and Horton left the valley on a pair of slow-moving horses.

"You shouldn't feel angry toward him," Horton said. "He's doing you a favor. It's best that you leave this jungle as quickly as possible. I've seen more than one person come here and start poking into the business of the Sengh Brotherhood. They usually don't live very long. If they do, they've been compromised.''

''What about the Jungle Patrol?'' If she couldn't get information out of the Phantom, maybe she'd have better luck with Horton. ''How do you deal with this brotherhood?''

''Very carefully. For the most part, we keep our distance. If they don't push us, we don't push them. It seems to work. It's the jungle way.''

Diana glanced back toward Skull Cave. She couldn't take her eyes off it, and hoped that the Phantom would make one more appearance.

She was upset, but she could hardly be angry with the Phantom. After all, he'd saved her life more than once yesterday. As far as she knew, he had no reason for lifting a finger to help her. That's what was truly amazing.

Horton noticed her looking back. ''Quite a fellow, isn't he?''

Diana just turned around and faced forward, her fingers touching the black pearls around her neck.

The Phantom headed directly to the Chronicle Chamber. He knew there was no point in arguing with Diana. She had no choice but to follow his wishes, and he was confident that she was in good hands with Horton. As long as she didn't do something stupid, like bolt away from him and try to investigate the Sengh Brotherhood on her own, she had a good chance of returning to New York alive.

Once in the Chronicle Chamber, he opened an old

steamer trunk and removed the top tray, revealing several items of clothing. He pulled out a tailored suit jacket, slacks, and an overcoat. He held them up, inspected them, and brushed them off.

"Looking for a change of wardrobe, Kit?"

The Phantom turned to see his father standing a few feet behind him. "The Sengh Brotherhood has spread to New York. I've got to do something about it. It's related to the skulls, too."

"It just goes from bad to worse," his father said. "They've always been confined to the jungle. Now they're loose in New York City. I agree, you must go there immediately, son."

"I am, Dad."

His father pointed to the suit Kit was holding. "Don't take the wool. You'll be sweating bullets."

"You're right." He was so used to receiving guidance from his father that it didn't even occur to him how odd it was that he was getting advice on what to wear from beyond the grave. He discarded the wool suit and packed a lighter one.

"I hate to say it, Kit, but it looks like the Brotherhood has the upper hand this time. Stay alert and follow your instincts. You *can* overcome the odds, but it won't be easy."

He turned to his father, whose expression seemed deeply sad, filled with regret. "I know that, Dad. That's why I'm going to New York."

It was past noon on the day after the fracas when Quill finally dragged himself back to the ship. He'd wandered in the jungle most of the night, uncertain which way would take him to the coast. He'd cursed the Phantom, the wolf, the woman, and all of his own useless men until he couldn't curse any more.

Finally around dawn, he'd come upon a riderless horse. He recognized it as one of the horses his men had borrowed from the village near the cove. Since the rider was missing, he figured the Phantom and the woman had managed to get away. For a brief moment, he'd thought about looking for the rider to find out what exactly had happened, but he quickly changed his mind. He didn't care what had happened. He needed to get back to the ship as quickly as possible.

Now that he was here, he headed directly to the crew quarters where he'd left his leather satchel with the silver skull. He spoke to no one as he raced through the ship, remembering that he'd stupidly left the satchel in plain view on a bunk.

He knew as soon as he saw it that it was empty. He hurried over to the bunk, ran his hands over the sides, unzipped it.

"Who the—"

"Hi, there, Quill," Sala said.

Sala was sitting cross-legged on another bunk. The skull was in her lap, and she was cleaning it with a toothbrush.

"Just what do you think you're doing?" He snatched the skull from her.

"Hey, take it easy. It rolled out of your bag. I was just cleaning it up and keeping an eye on it."

"It's mine."

"No it's not. It's the boss's, and he wants it right away. I decoded the message myself. I'm flying you to New York as soon as you get cleaned up."

"So everything's okay," Quill said. "I knew

it.'' He looked at the shiny skull. ''Nice job. How about coming into the shower now and helping me clean up? Remember, we were going to do that before.''

''Forget it. I must have been momentarily out of my mind. I'll meet you by the plane.''

TWENTY

New York City

Diana Palmer breezed into the city library and passed row after row of bookshelves and tables until she reached the reference desk in the history department. Behind it were several carts stacked with books and magazines, but no one was around. As she waited, her thoughts drifted back over the last couple of days.

Her arrival at La Guardia Airport had been nearly as exhausting as the long trip back. She'd been met by reporters and photographers, as well as Uncle Dave and her mother, who was crying with joy and berating Uncle Dave at the same time. It was a scene that had been repeated more than once, but this time Diana had a distinct feeling that arriving home safely didn't necessarily mean she was safe.

Uncle Dave was anxious to hear all the details. He and his reporters had gathered disturbing bits and pieces of the story after the Pan Am Clipper had been forced down into the Bangalla Sea. In fact, the *Tribune* had run a front-page article about it, prominently noting the kidnapping of the publisher's niece.

Diana told her story, at least a tempered version. She said her rescuer was a stranger and that she'd never found out who he really was—which, in a sense, was the truth. It was better that way, better for her and better for the Phantom. Privately she'd told Uncle Dave about the Sengh Brotherhood.

Now, a day later, the hoopla was over, and she could get down to work. "Excuse me," she said, waving a hand at a bespeckled young man who was prowling around in the stacks with a pile of books under his arms. "Can you help me with something?"

The librarian peered over his glasses at her, then carried his load of books up to the front desk where he set them down. He was thin and pale and his shoulders slumped, as if he'd been carrying too many books. He looked like he didn't want to be bothered. "What is it?"

"This is the reference desk, I believe," Diana said, annoyed by the man's attitude. "I'd like some help with research I'm doing on an organization called the Sengh Brotherhood." She spelled the name for him.

Diana was sure that whatever was available would cross-reference the material that Xander Drax had been studying. Somewhere in those documents would be a description of the supernatural force that Drax wanted to control.

"Well?" Diana asked impatiently.

The librarian, whose tiny, cheap name tag read Henri, said, "Recent or historical?"

"What?"

"I said, do you want recent or historical reference material?"

"Oh, both. I want everything you have."

Henri nodded and slipped away, as silent as a

ghost. He returned a few minutes later. The subject she was asking about was located in special collections and required her to fill out a request form that could only be approved by the director of the library. Then, after a pause, he added: "The director is not available today. I'm not sure when he will be available, either."

"My uncle, David Palmer, is a good friend of Dr. Fleming's. Maybe if I call him—"

"You mean, Mr. Palmer, the publisher of the *Tribune?*" Awe crept into his voice.

She nodded.

"I think you should speak to your uncle about Dr. Fleming. The *Tribune* is doing a story on his disappearance. It's really something of a mystery." He leaned forward. "We're really in the dark here. We don't know what's going on, except that the police are now involved, and they've been poking around here."

Diana remembered her uncle mentioning Xander Drax's secret research to the police commissioner and the mayor. "I'll tell you what, if you get me the material from special collections, I'll find out everything I can about the disappearance."

Henri pushed up his glasses, then looked to his right and left, making sure no one was listening to them. Then he smiled. "I suppose I can make an exception, especially since Dr. Fleming is unavailable."

Uncle Dave told her about Fleming. He was last seen leaving for a visit to Drax's office. Drax claimed he never showed up for the meeting, and the investigation was at a standstill. But one of his reporters had just talked to a clerk in a nearby cigar shop who had seen two men carrying something that looked like a body wrapped in a blanket to a Packard that was parked in an alley behind the building.

Diana passed on the information, taking care to avoid identifying the witness. She was all too well aware of Drax's ability to make witnesses and informers disappear. Henri looked disturbed by what he heard, but Diana was even more disturbed by what the librarian told her.

"I don't have very much for you," Henri confided. "Most of it is gone."

"What do you mean gone? Where is it?"

"Last night Police Commissioner Farley confiscated all the material that Xander Drax had requested during his visits. He said it was part of the investigation into Dr. Fleming's disappearance."

Or part of the coverup, Diana thought.

Henri pushed a cart over to a nearby table and carefully laid out three aged journals and several bound volumes of old newspapers. "This is all I have for you. Some of it dates back to the sixteenth century, so be very careful with it."

For the remainder of the morning and into the early afternoon, Diana studied the material. As she suspected, there was no mention of an ancient artifact of power. However, her research was not without some interesting discoveries.

The Sengh Brotherhood, she learned, was more than four centuries old. In the early fifteen hundreds, it was a well-trained fraternity of outlaws that attacked merchant ships. The Brotherhood was encountered on the Spanish main, the West Indies, and off the coast of Africa. But their headquarters and primary hunting grounds were believed to be the coastal region of Bangalla.

One newspaper article from the seventeenth century surprised Diana so much that she had to reread it twice. According to the report from the office of the governor of Jamaica, the Sengh Brotherhood had been destroyed by the legendary Phantom—and disbanded in 1612.

The same Phantom? Impossible, she thought. Maybe the Phantom she'd met was just someone imitating him. The other alternative was that "her Phantom" was a descendant of the original one. In other words, the Phantom could be a one-man tradition of sorts. One man, but also many men.

She prided herself on her knowledge of history, but more and more she was realizing that history was filled with obscure episodes that had faded into legend. Until a few days ago, she had never heard of either the Sengh Brotherhood or the Phantom. She probably never would've heard of them, either, except for one odd fact that seemed to contradict the article. Both the Brotherhood and the Phantom had survived to this day.

She sensed someone standing beside her and jerked her head around to see the librarian. "Oh, Henri, you startled me," she said, placing a hand below her throat. "I'm just about done here."

"Take your time. I won't be leaving for another hour and a half. Meanwhile, is there anything else I can get for you?"

Gee, after his slow start, Henri had become impressively cooperative. "No, I don't think— Wait a minute." She showed him the article that mentioned the Phantom. "Can you look for something about this Phantom?"

He pushed up his glasses and read the article. "The Phantom, hmm. Sounds like a legend. But I'll see what I can find."

Diana continued reading and found out that the report from Jamaica had been inaccurate. Later records referred to acts of piracy by the Sengh Brotherhood in the early eighteenth century in east Africa, in 1818 near Suez, and the final recorded sighting was off the coast of China in the spring of 1898.

"Well, I did find something for you," Henri said. "I hope this helps."

He handed her an oversized book called *The Mythical Heros of All Times.* The Phantom was included in a chapter entitled "Modern Legends." She read that the legend originated in the early part of the sixteenth century and was about a mysterious masked hero whose face was never seen. The Phantom's father had been killed by pirates, and he had grown up vowing to fight worldwide piracy.

Diana read on. "The battle against this nemesis to civilization, though, was so vast that it necessarily extended beyond one lifetime, and so the Phantom was also known as The Ghost Who Walks and The Man Who Cannot Die."

The author suggested that the legend was based on an actual person who lived in the latter part of the sixteenth century and early seventeenth century. "In 1612 the Phantom battled a band of vicious pirates known as 'the Sengh Brothers.' He succeeded in killing their leader, Brunel de Gottschalk, then he blew up the powder magazine in the band's castle, destroying their stronghold.

"While there is no historical figure known as the Phantom, the remains of the castle he destroyed can still be found on the coast of Bangalla, where the native peoples are convinced that the Phantom remains alive deep in the Bangalla jungle. 'The Phantom is dead; long live the Phantom' is a popular saying among the primitive tribes of Bangalla."

Diana repeated the saying to herself as she closed the book. She thought about her time with the Phantom in his Deep Woods hideout and wondered if she would ever see him again. She felt that she would, but perhaps that was nothing but wishful thinking.

"Did that help you?" Henri asked.

She looked up. "Yes, but I think the article needs to be revised and updated." She thought about what she'd read and about what she knew. "Then again, maybe it's best just the way it is."

She stood up, thanked Henri, and left. She felt intrigued by what she had discovered, but disappointed by what she had not. She headed directly to the *Tribune* building. She needed to tell her uncle that Commissioner Farley had confiscated the critical records.

TWENTY-ONE

Xander Drax felt like a little kid at Christmas. He couldn't take his eyes off the leather satchel. What he really wanted to do was run his hands over it, feel the shape of his precious cargo, but he wasn't alone in his office. Seated opposite him were Quill and Sala, two recent additions to his entourage of loyal workhorses.

Drax finally leaned forward and reached into the satchel. His hands slipped over the smooth dome of the silver Skull of Touganda. What a texture it had, he thought, a silken coolness, a kind of vibrancy.

He lifted the skull out of the satchel and held it up in the light. "Oh, baby. Come to papa. It's beautiful. Just beautiful."

"I used a little toothpaste. It polished up real nice," Sala said.

Drax gave her a cold look that made it clear she wasn't to touch it. She had no idea, no idea whatsoever, of what she was dealing with. But he decided not to comment. He put the skull back in the satchel.

"I'm in such a good mood right now, I almost hate to mention this minor matter, but . . ." He picked up the newspaper and turned it around so they could

read the top headline: EDITOR'S NIECE ESCAPES KIDNAP-
PERS—DIANA PALMER RETURNS HOME. Below the head-
line was a photograph of Diana being embraced by
David Palmer.

"The happy homecoming. Brings tears to your
eyes, doesn't it?" He looked from Sala to Quill. "So,
what went wrong?"

They both started talking at the same time. Then
Sala let Quill speak: "Something we didn't count on.
It was a total surprise."

"And what was that?" Drax asked, tapping a pencil against his desk.

"The Phantom."

Drax frowned. "I thought that nonsense was just
a superstition—native bugaboo."

"Oh, no. He's real," Quill insisted. "And he won't
die. I know. I killed him once, I mean twice . . . and
he isn't dead."

"That doesn't make sense." Drax's impatience
leaked into his voice. He dropped his pencil and
rested his chin on his folded hands as he stared at
Quill. "Start at the beginning."

"Look, I brought this to prove it." Quill opened
his coat, revealing a skull-head holster around his
waist, exactly like the one the Phantom wore. He
unbuckled it, slid it off, and held it up.

"See this hole? This is where I stuck him ten years
ago with a twelve-inch blade."

"You stabbed him in the back?" Drax smiled.
"I've underestimated you, Quill."

Quill beamed. "Right to the hilt."

"It's not the story I heard," Sala said dryly.

"That should've done the trick, all right," Drax

said, reassessing the situation. "So what happened the second time?"

Quill told him how he'd stabbed him in the side, about the rope bridge, and the gorge. "I saw the truck fall, and I never saw him get out of it. I was there. I tell you, he's invincible."

"The Phantom helped Diana to escape," Sala said. "I think he's in love with her."

Drax rolled his eyes. "Really, this is getting more interesting by the second. Maybe he's not quite so invincible. Love is a great weakness. We can always take advantage of it." He looked at Sala. "What makes you think he's in love?"

"Because he could've had me. He picked her. It can only be love."

Drax looked her over as though she were an apple he was about to eat. Sala seemed more than willing to be the apple of his eye. She leaned forward, her pose hardly provocative despite her best attempts to make it seem so. "Maybe it was just bad judgment on his part."

"What should we do about him?" Quill asked.

"Nothing for now," Drax answered. "This is New York City. I'm not concerned about some jungle folk-hero half a world away."

Kit Walker stepped out of a taxicab in the heart of Manhattan. He was wearing a tailored suit and dark glasses. It had been several years since he'd been in New York, and he knew from past experiences that it took him a while to adjust to the crowds and the buildings.

He casually handed the taxi driver several bills. "Keep the change."

"Thank you very much, sir," the cabbie replied.

When he traveled, he was a chameleon who fit in wherever he went. But it had been some time since he'd been out of the jungle, and he hoped it didn't show. For a moment, he thought, he was doing quite well. But the cab driver wasn't fooled.

"Hey, not so fast!" He jumped out and ran around his cab, waving Kit's money. "What is this? It's not real money."

"You're right. That's Bangallan currency."

"Coin of the realm would be much appreciated," the driver replied dryly.

Kit fished into his pocket. "I'm afraid it's all I've got on me."

"It better not be."

"Wait! Here's something," Kit said, reaching into another pocket. "These are opals. And this one looks like a star sapphire." He held it up to the light and nodded. And these other ones ... oh here, take them all."

The chunky driver, who had talked all the way from the airport, was momentarily at a loss for words as Kit dropped the gems into his palm.

"Don't worry. They're real," Kit said. "And they should buy your services for the rest of the day—so wait right here."

"You're kidding. . . ."

"I never kid."

Kit walked into a building that said *New York Tribune* above the door.

About the same time that Kit was arriving at the *Tribune* building, a few blocks away Drax was convening a meeting in his office, high above street level. Seated at the table were Police Commissioner Farley, Quill, and Sala, and the Zephro brothers, Raymond and Charlie.

Drax stood in front of the group and pressed a button. The drapes closed automatically and the room faded to black. As it did he opened the meeting with three words: "Darkness rules the earth!"

Drax let the words sink in, then continued: "But don't take my word for it. Just look around. America is in financial ruin and Europe and Asia are on the brink of self-annihilation. Armies clash in the night. Governments crumble. Borders dissolve. Nations vanish. Chaos reigns. But like I've always said: there is opportunity in chaos. Lots of opportunity."

Then he reached into the leather satchel and removed the silver skull. "And so, my brothers, I give you the Skull of Touganda!"

Drax hit a button on his desk. A glass slide projector lit up and beamed the image of two skulls on the wall. "This skull is one of three. When all three are united, they will produce a force more powerful than any army on earth, a force like the world has never seen."

He walked over to the wall and held the silver skull between the two images that were projected on the wall, symbolically uniting the three. The eyes in the silver skull seemed to glow, creating an eerie, malefic effect that wasn't lost on anyone in the room.

Raymond Zephro broke the spell. "But you only have the one."

"Legend has it that if the skulls are separated, two of the skulls will point the way to the third one," Drax explained.

"Like I said, you only—"

Drax cut him off. "But I know the location of the second skull."

Everyone perked up at that bit of information. They looked around, exchanging glances. Then Drax hit a button and the spider-web symbol was projected on the wall.

"You're looking at the symbol of the Sengh Brotherhood, a confederation of evil that has marauded exotic regions of the globe for more than four centuries. We shall succeed where they have failed. They have pointed the way, but we will complete the journey. The skulls—and the power that comes with them—shall be ours."

"Wait a minute," Raymond Zephro interrupted. "What makes you believe any of this power stuff is true? That sounds like a superstition, if you ask me."

"Good point," Drax said. "But I've done my research. I've looked into the past, and I know there were objects with great powers that have been lost for many centuries. The Skulls of Touganda were among the most powerful. The prophecies of the Tougandan shamans said that the skulls would be lost, then one day reunited and their powers would be multiplied."

"Don't you think the Sengh Brotherhood is going to be interested in those skulls?" Quill asked.

"When I bring the skulls together, the Sengh Brotherhood will be totally irrelevant."

Drax hit another button and a new symbol replaced the large spider web on the screen. It was a large X with smaller letters—D-R-A—fitted snugly around it. The DRAX logo.

Raymond Zephro leaped to his feet. "Count me out. It's wrong! Skulls, forces of darkness—it isn't right! I was an altar boy, for the love of Pete! At St. Timothy's. So were you, Charlie. This isn't right. We weren't raised like this.''

"Sit down, Ray," Drax said.

"The only 'power' I believe in comes out of the barrel of a gun, not from some jungle souvenirs." Raymond Zephro turned to his brother. "So, what's the story? Are you with me, Charlie?''

Charlie Zephro was quiet a moment. When he spoke, his voice was firm. "You're on your own, Ray.''

"Fine. Suit yourself." Raymond Zephro headed to the door, where he paused. "But I'm gone, Drax. And I'm taking my entire syndicate with me!''

"If that's how you feel about it, Ray.''

As Ray turned his back, Drax whirled around swiftly, grabbed an African spear from the wall, and hurled it at the traitor. The spear found its mark between Raymond Zephro's shoulder blades. It pierced his body, knocked him forward, and pinned him to the wall. He jerked and twitched for a few seconds, then went limp. No one in the room moved or spoke.

"Anyone else feel like leaving?" Drax asked.

Silence.

"Good. I do *so* hate interruptions." Drax rubbed his right shoulder, working out the stiffness. "The bursitis seems to be flaring up again." He turned to the remaining Zephro brother. "Charlie, you're the new boss of bosses. Can you handle it?''

Charlie beamed, already over the shock of his brother's sudden violent death. "Been waiting all my life.''

Jack Farley looked as if he were undergoing some sort of personal crisis. He was shifting uneasily in his chair, his head was wobbling from side to side, he kept blinking his eyes. He was obviously having difficulty maintaining his composure.

But he was police commissioner, an eye witness to a murder, and he couldn't do anything about it. He was far too indebted to Drax, and afraid of him. But finally he regained his poise.

"Uh, Xander, the plans have been set for tonight to go in and get the item while the building is closed."

"No," Drax said. "I can't wait that long. This is too exciting. We go in now."

"What? In the middle of the afternoon?" Farley started to lose his composure again. He looked as if he'd just realized he was standing naked in front of an audience of critics.

"Yes." Drax circled the table and walked behind Farley. "And I'd appreciate it if you'd keep your policemen away until I'm done. Is that understood?"

"I'll see what I can do," Farley muttered, and wiped his brow.

Drax called an end to the meeting.

Diana Palmer moved through the lobby of the newspaper building at a rapid clip. But not rapid enough to avoid Jimmy Wells.

"Hey, found you! The page-one girl! Back from her escapade in the jungle."

Diana continued walking. She didn't feel like talking to Jimmy just now, but she didn't want to offend him, either. "Jimmy, what're you doing here?"

"I was in town on business. I thought we could get together for a while."

"What business?" She was curious to know if Jimmy was actually working.

"I was having some suits made," he said, sounding slightly annoyed and defensive.

"That's not business." She turned down a hallway, and Jimmy followed.

"It is for the guy making the suits," he said brightly. "Why do you have to be so difficult? I just thought we could grab an early dinner and a show. What do you say?"

"Can I take a rain check?"

"Sure. Add it to your collection."

Jimmy sounded defeated, yet he always bounced back quickly. He never gave up on her. Maybe it was arrogance, maybe it was just plain stubbornness. In some ways he was like an endearing little pet.

She turned into her uncle's office with Jimmy still tagging along. Uncle Dave was at the front desk consulting with his secretary. He looked pleased to see her. "Diana, I have a surprise for you. Come into my office."

Diana followed him into the room. A tall man with broad shoulders was standing by the window, looking out onto the street. He turned and met her gaze.

"Kit! What a surprise!"

"Hello, Diana. It's been awhile, hasn't it?"

"A few years at least."

He looked just as handsome as she remembered— the same square jaw, bold features, and dark, compelling eyes. Kit had been the greatest passion of her life, and then an even greater disappointment. Now here he was again, and her feelings about him were once again in conflict as it all came back.

"Six to be exact," he said. "I read about what happened. Are you okay?"

"I'm fine. It started out bad, but it turned out all right."

If there was time, she would like to tell him about it. She figured he would be interested. She remembered him as someone who was always willing to take a chance to help someone or right a wrong, even when doing so put him at personal risk. But she had something else to talk to him about before she told him anything about her present life. She needed to know what had happened to him, why he'd simply disappeared.

Jimmy had been totally ignored, so he stepped forward and introduced himself. "By the way, Jimmy Wells. Nice to meet you."

"Kit Walker."

"So, tell me, Kit, I'm curious, where do you know our Diana from?"

"We were friends at college."

"I see."

Diana could tell Jimmy was mulling over the word "friends," wondering exactly what that meant. "Are you living here in New York?" she asked.

"No. Just passing through. Your Uncle Dave and I have been catching up on old times."

"And trading information about Xander Drax," Uncle Dave added.

"What do you know about Drax?" Diana was curious about what had brought Kit here, but even more interested in finding out what he knew about Drax.

"Drax has come into possession of a rare artifact connected to the Sengh Brotherhood," Uncle Dave said, answering for Kit. Then he turned to Kit and encouraged him to tell Diana what he knew.

"Yes. It's an ancient silver skull with precious jewels where the eyes and teeth would be."

"Oh, yeah," Jimmy said, casually. "I've seen something like that before."

"You have?" Kit suddenly took a renewed interest in Jimmy.

"Yeah. But it wasn't silver. I think it was black," he explained.

"Black? Black jade, perhaps. Where did you see it, Jimmy?"

"Let's see. It was my twelfth birthday party. Mom and Dad rented this big room. Oh, now I remember." He looked around, basking in the sudden attention. All eyes were on him. "The Museum of Natural History."

TWENTY-TWO

The cabby was leaning against his taxicab when he spotted Kit walking away from the *Tribune* building. He straightened up and opened the back door like he was a limo driver. "Yes, sir. At your service," he said with a snappy salute.

Kit was taken aback by the man's new attitude. "I see you're in a good mood."

"You bet I am," the cabby beamed. "While you were inside, I had those stones appraised. And you can call me Al. Rhymes with pal."

Diana hurried out of the building and rushed up to Kit. "I'm going with you," she said, and slid into the back of the cab before he could object.

"You don't even know where—"

"Yes, I do."

"Where to now, sir?"

"Museum of Natural History," Diana said quickly.

The cabby turned to Kit for confirmation.

"You heard the lady," Kit said.

"Yes, sir."

"You know him?" Diana asked.

"I just met him."

"And he's ready to zip you around town."

"Apparently."

"I don't get it," she murmured.

Moments later Kit and Diana were speeding through the concrete corridors of midtown Manhattan. "You haven't changed a bit, Diana. You look ... well, great. Prettier than ever."

"You just vanished, Kit. You never even said good-bye, or said where you were going."

Kit's smile faded. Time to pay the piper, he thought. "I guess you're right."

"That's all you can say? You never even sent a letter, never called, nothing. You just disappeared."

"I know." He'd told her he'd grown up overseas and might return there after graduating. When she'd asked where exactly he'd grown up, he'd been vague. He said he'd moved around because of his father's business dealings, which he couldn't talk about.

"Why?"

"I had to go home," Kit said. "My father died rather suddenly."

"I'm sorry about your dad. But it wasn't fair that you never bothered getting in touch with me. It was the least you could have done." She crossed her arms and looked out the window as the taxicab turned down Fifth Avenue.

"I had to take over the family business. It's hard to explain, but I've thought about you a lot since then, Diana."

"I thought about you too, Kit. Then I stopped and went on with my life."

"I know. Dave brought me up to date. One adventure after another."

"What about you, Kit? Tell me about this family

business. What exactly do you do? Are you a spy, an international art thief, or a jewel thief, what?''

Kit noticed the cabby raise his head when he heard that last possibility. ''No. Nothing like it. At least, nothing illegal.''

''Then what is it?''

''The family business? Well, it's . . .''

''What? A little hard to explain?''

''As a matter of fact, it is. Sometimes there are jewels involved and sometimes there's spying involved, too. But I'm not a jewel thief and I'm not a spy.''

Diana shook her head, resigned to the fact that he wasn't going to tell her any more than that. ''You always were a mystery, Kit.''

He pointed to her necklace. ''Those are certainly unusual.''

''Stop changing the subject.''

She was pouting now. He had always liked her face when she pouted; liked it when she didn't, too.

''They look valuable,'' he went on.

''They're black pearls.''

''Really? Where would you get something like that, I wonder?''

''It was a gift.''

''From somebody special?''

Diana didn't answer. He could tell she didn't know what to say.

''That's okay. I understand.''

She shook her head and laughed. ''You can't possibly understand. I don't even understand it myself.''

''Well, I guess I had my chance.''

''I guess you did.''

They both fell silent. After a couple more blocks,

the cabby pulled over to the curb. "Here we are, Mr. Walker. The museum."

En route to the skull display, they wove their way from room to room, past artifacts from dimly remembered centuries and dead civilizations. It all blurred together for Diana, who was still puzzling over Kit's unwillingness to talk about himself. Why was she attracted to these mystery men, anyway? They only left her baffled and frustrated. Yet, the attraction was undeniable.

"Over here," Kit said, motioning toward a glass-encased display.

Diana stared in awe at the black jade skull with its jewel-encrusted eye sockets. It was on display in a huge diorama, which depicted a scene from the crusades: Christian soldiers battling Saracen warriors.

"This is really fascinating," she said. "I had no idea of the historical context."

But Kit was frowning. "They've got it all wrong. Incredible. Wrong century. Wrong hemisphere. Wrong culture. This skull hasn't been lost; it's just been misplaced. *Badly* misplaced."

How did he know? Diana wondered. Kit Walker stepped into her life after six years and knew exactly what she was trying to find out about Xander Drax. Now he knew the history of this black skull apparently better than the historians.

"What's your interest in Drax and these skulls?" she asked, not really expecting a direct answer.

But he surprised her. "I represent the true owners of the skulls. I want to see them returned, and Drax wants them for himself."

"Simple as that, huh?"

"Yes."

"Why does Drax want them?" She had the feeling she already knew the answer, but she wanted to hear what Kit had to say.

"Because he's discovered a very ancient secret," Kit whispered, fingers pressed against the glass. "The three Skulls of Touganda are the source of ultimate and absolute power."

Diana looked around the room. "I traveled all the way to the Bangalla jungle, nearly got myself killed, and the answer was right here under my nose? Incredible."

"We can't let Drax get his hands on this skull. I've got to get it out of here."

She peered at him as if he'd lost his mind. Well, maybe he had. Maybe the only mystery about Kit was that he was a bit daft. "And just how do you propose to do that?"

Kit made a fist as if he were about to smash the display, when Diana reached out and grabbed his arm. "Wait. There's a safer way. Uncle Dave knows an important member on the board of directors. It might take a day or two, but I'm sure that something could be . . ."

As she spoke, Kit slipped out of her light grasp and grabbed a heavy pedestal. He swung it like a baseball bat and smashed it against the glass. An alarm shrieked.

"Or we could just break the glass," she muttered.

Kit stepped over the jagged edges of glass, grabbed the jade skull. Diana knew they were in trouble from the moment the alarm sounded. But she didn't realize what kind of trouble. As Kit slipped out of the diorama, several men rushed into the room.

One of them was Drax and another was the thug from the jungle, Quill. They were backed up by several gangster types, no doubt from the Zephro Brothers organization. Quill grabbed her and pulled her arms around her back

"Give that to me," Drax ordered, pointing at the skull in Kit's hands.

One of the gangsters snatched the skull from his grasp and stuffed it into a leather satchel. Diana recognized him as Charlie Zephro, from pictures in the newspaper. Uncle Dave had tried to expose the Zephros more than once.

A crowd was gathering in the room as the alarm continued to blare. Drax, dressed impeccably in a black suit turned to the crowd. "Museum security. Everything is under control." He held up his hands, patting the air, and smiled. "Free cake and sandwiches are being served in the Hall of Nature. Don't miss it."

Diana wondered where the real security people were. Then she quickly figured out that Drax had probably paid off someone to get rid of the security people, the police, anyone who would stop him. Like he told Uncle Dave, he usually got what he wanted.

As the crowd dispersed, Drax turned to Kit. "Who are *you*?"

"Just a fellow collector, Mr. Drax."

Diana saw light emanating from the satchel. As she stared at it, she realized she could actually see through the satchel. Inside was not one skull but two. Drax had the silver and jade skulls.

"Hey, Drax, the bag!" Charlie Zephro held it up. "The damn things got lights."

Then the bag started to smoke and Charlie dropped

it on the floor. Drax scooped out the skulls, clutching one in either hand. The skulls slammed together as though they were drawn by a strong magnetic force.

"Something's happening!" Drax shouted. "This is it! It's happening right here and now!"

The eyes of the two skulls began to glow, to pulse with colors. Native drums pounded loudly, surrounding them with sound. The room seemed to vibrate. Huge shadows of jungle palms danced across the walls. The overhead lights flashed off and on and off again. Smoke and mist swirled in the air as chaos erupted in the room—screams, shouts, people flinging themselves to the floor.

Drax stayed on his feet; he stood straight in the middle of it all, electrified by the sight, marveling at the wonder. Diana was petrified, but nonetheless fascinated by what she was witnessing.

"Unbelievable! It's beautiful. It's magnificent. Show me the power! Show me the power!" As Drax spoke, stained-glass windows high overhead shattered one after another. "Amazing!"

Just when it seemed that the show of power would go no further, rays of light shot from the skulls' eyes. The drumming built to a crescendo, and the beams converged on the wall. One particular spot on the wall was so blindingly bright, Diana had to squint to keep watching. But the brightness grew until it pierced her eyes, forcing her to shut them. Then, suddenly, unexpectedly, the sound, the light, the entire exhibition of power, abruptly stopped. Everything was calm again.

For seconds there was nothing but stillness in the room. Then people staggered to their feet like survivors of some terrible natural disaster, a hurricane, a tornado, crippling hail.

Zephro's goons lunged for Kit and Diana and pinned their arms behind their backs.

Quill was the first one to walk over to the wall. ''Look!''

The beams of light had struck a mural map of the world, and burned what looked like the shape of a skull into the map. From where she stood, it appeared that the spot was located in the middle of the ocean.

''The skulls have spoken!'' Drax shouted triumphantly. He held his arms out with his palms upturned and dropped his head back, as if claiming the entire universe as his new domain.

Diana and Kit exchanged a glance, then were hustled out of the room, surrounded by Zephro's goons.

TWENTY-THREE

Kit and Diana were shoved into the backseat of a luxurious Pierce-Arrow in front of the museum. The cabby was watching the entire scenario, and as they pulled away, Kit saw the driver jump into his cab and follow them at a discreet distance.

The ride lasted less than five minutes. Just seconds after the Pierce-Arrow stopped, Quill and three gangsters pulled Kit and Diana out of the car and hurried them into a nearby office building. The thugs formed a tight circle around them in the elevator. No one spoke as they rose to the twenty-fourth floor. Then they were escorted into a huge, plush office and forcefully seated in straight-back chairs.

"What do you think is going to happen now?" Diana asked quietly, her voice nervous.

Kit noticed the symbol of the Drax Corporation on the wall, verifying what he already suspected, that they'd been taken to Drax's headquarters. "Drax is going to interrogate us, then his goons will beat me up. Or maybe his goons will beat me up first. That remains to be seen."

"Shut up!" one of the Zephro gangsters said.

A moment later, Drax, Quill, and Zephro entered

the office. Drax didn't waste any time. He stopped in front of him. "What's your name? And why were you trying to steal the skull?"

"Kit Walker."

"What about the skull?"

"I thought it would go well with my new drapes."

"You're cute, Mr. Walker. Fortunately, I have a cure for that."

Drax nodded to Zephro, who jerked Kit from the chair and twisted his arms behind his back. At the same time, Quill drove his fist deep into Kit's stomach, knocking the wind out of him and possibly rearranging his organs.

Kit sank to his knees and saw the Phantom skullhead gun belt around Quill's waist. He touched his own gun belt beneath his suit just to make sure he was still wearing it.

"Stop it!" Diana yelled. "Don't hurt him."

"Why, Diana Palmer, are you sweet on Mr. Walker? I thought your true love was swinging on a jungle vine somewhere."

"How did you know about—" She stopped. "I mean, what makes you think that?"

"I told him," a woman's voice said from the corner of the office.

Kit turned his head as Sala got up from a couch and stepped forward.

"Sala's got all the latest gossip on two continents," Drax said, sounding amused.

"Go ahead, deny it," Sala said. "But you know he's in love with you and you're nuts about him. From the moment he came flying out of that laundry chute, you were hooked on the purple guy."

"Kismet in the jungle," Drax said.

"You're despicable," Diana snapped at Drax. She turned to Sala. "And you're just jealous."

Sala slapped her across the face. "Now I'm one up on you."

Drax motioned to Quill. "Take Mr. Walker up to the observation deck and make him talk."

"I claim the body when you're done," Sala said, and laughed.

Quill and several other men jerked Kit to his feet and dragged him out of the office. They led him down a hall. Kit was slumped forward and wobbling. He made no effort to resist his captors. As they turned up a stairwell, he stumbled and was pulled to his feet. And then he reacted.

He spun around and kicked Quill in the chest. Quill stumbled back into two of the thugs and continued to tumble down the stairs, taking the two men with him. Kit dashed up the steps and ducked into a utility room. It was dark and full of vents and ducts and air shafts, and at one end was a giant fan. Quickly he shed his suit jacket, shirt, and pants and pressed up against a wall as he heard footsteps.

Quill and the gangsters entered the utility room with their guns drawn. "He must be in here." Quill signaled them to split up as they moved forward.

The thugs moved to the center of the room where they came upon a pile of clothes heaped on the floor. They picked through the clothes like vultures looking for carrion and realized they belonged to Kit. They looked baffled.

"Hey, now what's this supposed to mean?" one of them asked.

That's when the Phantom stepped out from behind them and knocked their heads together. The two men slumped to the floor. The Phantom glanced across the room just as Quill spotted him.

"What the . . . !" Quill raised his weapon and fired wildly. Then he dashed for the door as if the room were about to exploded.

The Phantom grabbed the doorknob, but Quill had locked it from the outside. Realizing what was about to happen, the Phantom dove to the side. Bullets cracked through the door, ricocheting wildly about the room.

The Phantom figured that the only other way out was through the duct system. But to get into it, he had to enter through the giant fan. When the firing ceased, he pulled off the cover. The rapidly rotating blades were at least five feet in diameter.

He tried to jam the fan blades with a broom handle, but the blades chopped the handle into splinters. The Phantom drew one of his pistols and, with extraordinary concentration and strength, suddenly plunged it into the spinning fan. He squeezed hard to keep the pistol from being ripped from his hand. Sparks flew, but the blades finally stopped turning.

With his free hand, he took off his gun belt and quickly looped it around one of the blades. Then he carefully slipped between the blades and into the duct. Finally he jerked his gun belt away from the fan, and it whirred to life again.

Drax unrolled a large map across his desk. He was still excited by what had happened at the museum, and was no longer concerned about Diana or Kit. Diana realized that she had ceased to exist for Drax, but Charlie Zephro was standing behind her, guarding her like a hyena with its wounded prey, ready to act if she tried anything.

"Once I check the coordinates from that map in the museum against this navigational chart, we'll have the location of the third skull," Drax said.

Sala moved around the desk and held one end of the map down so it didn't curl inward. Drax, meanwhile, kept mulling over the map, searching for the coordinates. "Ah, here we go. Isn't this interesting?"

"Where is it?" Zephro asked. "I hope it ain't under the water, because I can't swim."

Drax ignored him. "The Devil's Vortex. We're going to the Devil's Vortex. Let's get ready. No time to waste."

"Are you sure?" Sala asked. Check again. Maybe you made a mistake."

"No mistake."

"Isn't that the place where all those ships keep disappearing?" Zephro asked.

"Yes. Incredible, isn't it?" Drax stepped back from the map, placing his hands on his hips. But his gaze never left the fabled vortex. "There must be an island there, an uncharted island."

"I certainly hope so," Zephro said, then thinking it over, he added: "Maybe my brother was right about all this stuff."

"Nonsense. Where's your spirit of adventure?" Drax walked over to Zephro and put his arm over his shoulder. "Get Commissioner Farley on the phone. We need to get out of town as quickly as possible."

Zephro nodded, but didn't look very enthused. "Yeah. Okay."

Diana listened to it all. But her thoughts were on

Kit's fate and ultimately her own. The chances that Drax was going to let them live weren't very good. Even though she was Dave Palmer's niece, that wasn't going to stop him. After all, he hadn't hesitated making Dr. Fleming disappear, even though the library director's last appointment was known to be with Drax.

While Zephro made the call, Drax and Sala carried on about their upcoming adventure in the Caribbean, and she was cozying up to him. Diana knew it was time to take a chance. She slowly positioned herself, mustered her nerve, and leaped for the door.

She pulled it open and rushed past Drax's startled secretary, then through another doorway and out into the hall. She glanced right, left, decided to go right. She dashed down the corridor as she heard raised voices and chaos coming from Drax's office.

Diana reached the stairs, hesitated, then dashed up the flight of steps. She had to help Kit, and hopefully the two of them would escape.

Her decision fooled Zephro and Drax, who raced down the stairs, expecting her to attempt to escape the building by the quickest route. But then she heard footsteps behind her and knew that Sala hadn't been fooled.

Diana ran past the open utility room door and continued up to the observation deck. As she burst out onto the deck, it only took a moment to realize that Drax had been referring to the roof. By now Quill and the other thugs might have tossed Kit over the side.

She looked around, but didn't see anyone. She moved around the enclosure that covered the elevator shaft, but there was no sign of him there, either. *Where are you, Kit? Where?*

Then Sala stepped out. "I know you're up here, Diana. C'mon out, c'mon out, wherever you are!" she called in a soft, singsong voice.

Diana crept along the side of the enclosure. She saw Sala, pistol in hand, six or seven feet away—two steps and a lunge. She was about to make her move when Sala spun around.

"There you are, Diana!" She smiled. "You didn't really think you were going to save your buddy and get away, did you?"

"Listen, Sala. You don't have to go along with Drax. He's only going to get you in a lot of trouble. He's already gotten you into trouble."

Sala smiled sweetly. "How nice of you to be concerned about my welfare, Diana. But don't forget, I'm already in big trouble. Remember those laws I broke for bringing down the Pan Am Clipper? And for kidnapping you."

"You haven't exactly been a good girl, but—"

"But there's always time to reform, right?"

"That's right."

"Well, sorry, but I don't think this is the right time," Sala said. "Now let's go back downstairs, and everything will be forgiven. Sort of."

Diana held her ground.

Sala took a step closer. "Hey, I ain't kidding here. You got no choice in the matter."

Play it her way for now, Diana thought. "Okay." She walked toward Sala and the doorway to the stairs.

"That's better. I'll tell Drax you came up for a little fresh air."

Suddenly Diana's hand shot out and she grabbed Sala's wrist and twisted. The gun went off, slipped from Sala's grasp, and hit the floor. This time Diana scooped it up, but Sala grabbed her arm. They struggled, and the gun fired again, this time skyward.

Diana stepped out with her foot, tripped Sala, and they both tottered and fell to the roof. They rolled over and over, struggling for the gun, rolling closer to the edge of the roof until they were one revolution short of spinning into space.

Sala ended up on top, but now Diana had the gun, and she jammed the barrel right between Sala's eyes. "Just take it easy, Sala. I don't want to blow your head off, but I will if I have to."

"Go ahead," a voice said behind her. Then Drax laughed. "You shoot her, then I shoot you." He pressed his pistol against Diana's forehead. "Then you know what we've got? A bloody mess, but two less mouths to feed on our trip to the vortex."

"Drax, don't tell her to shoot me! I'm with you." Sala pleaded.

"It's survival of the fittest, sweetheart. It looks to me like you lost your chance to shoot." Then to Diana, he said, "Either shoot her or put the gun down. Make up your mind."

Diana dropped the gun. Drax grabbed it, and Sala jerked Diana to her feet. She pulled back her fist and was about to slam it into Diana's mouth when Drax pointed her own gun at her. "You knock her out and you're carrying her."

Sala lowered her fist and scowled at Diana. "We have quite a relationship, you and me."

"Hey, where's Quill and the others?" Drax said,

looking around as Charlie Zephro stopped at the top of the stairs. "What did he do with Walker?"

"I didn't see any of them," Zephro said.

"Then c'mon. Let's go find them."

Drax led the way downstairs, and just as they reached the bank of elevators, Quill turned a corner at the far end of the hall and loped toward them. At that same moment, one of the elevator doors opened and Commissioner Farley, accompanied by a middle-aged uniformed cop, stepped out.

"Mr. Drax, I've made all the arrangements. You're getting a full police escort."

"Excellent," Drax responded. "Have you heard the news? We're going to the Devil's Vortex."

Quill couldn't contain himself any longer. "Drax. The Phantom's here! He's in the building!"

"What?"

"I saw him with my own two eyes, mask and hood and purple getup."

The Phantom? Diana was confused, then amazed. She'd thought that nothing he did could surprise her anymore, but he'd done it again. He must have realized that Quill was bringing the silver skull to Drax and followed him here. But what happened to Kit?

Drax instantly turned to Farley. "Alert your officers. Tell them there's a madman on the loose. He's extremely dangerous." He glanced at Diana. "And tell them to shoot him on sight."

"Don't worry about a thing," Farley said, and turned to the cop at his side. "Sergeant, you heard him. Alert everyone on the street."

Drax motioned to Zephro and Sala. "Let's go. We've got a plane to catch."

"What about the girl?" Zephro said.

"Bring her! She's our 'Phantom insurance'!"

The door to an elevator opened and they all piled inside.

Good luck, Phantom. Good luck, Kit, Diana thought.

TWENTY-FOUR

Moments after Drax and his entourage, with Diana in tow, disappeared into the elevator, the Phantom pushed out a vent from the ceiling and dropped down into the hallway. All of the elevators were in use, so he tried to pry open the doors of one of them with his fingers. The panels slid slowly apart, exposing the empty shaft.

He peered down into the dark hole, then leaped onto the elevator cable. It was freshly greased and he slid fast, then faster and faster. The floors flew past him, his hands literally smoking.

Then he looked up and to his surprise saw the elevator cage speeding down toward him. Where had it come from? Then he realized it must have been on the observation deck. The cage was gaining on him as he raced toward the bottom of the shaft. He arrived only seconds ahead of it, pried open the doors, and tumbled into the lobby just as the cage slowed to a stop.

In front of the building, Drax and company were climbing into the Pierce-Arrow, which was surrounded by a police motorcycle escort. The Phantom rushed from the building just in time to see the motorcade start down Fifth Avenue.

He glanced around and spotted the cabby's taxi parked at the curb. He rushed over to the taxi and slid into the backseat. The startled cabby gaped at the Phantom. "What the hell?"

"Hi, Al. Thanks for being there."

"*Who* are you?"

"I'm a friend of Kit Walker's, and I need your help right now."

The Phantom looked up as a police officer approached the cab. He slid across the seat and out the opposite door. The street was clogged with traffic, so the Phantom jumped from one car to another, climbing from car roof to car roof, from hood to hood. Finally he leaped from a car roof and into the saddle of a mounted policeman's horse.

"Hey!" shouted the cop, who was writing a ticket.

He blew his whistle and two cops on motorcycles pulled away from the curb in pursuit. The Phantom galloped down the sidewalk, and pedestrians dove for cover as the motorcycles followed close behind. At the next break in the wall that separated the famous avenue from Central Park, the Phantom jerked the reins right and galloped into the park.

He followed a footpath, the motorcycles still behind him and gaining. He rode through a cluster of trees, back onto the path, and over a stone bridge. The cops, in close pursuit now, fired their guns. The Phantom ducked as bullets whistled overhead.

Finally he leaped from the horse and landed on a large boulder. He scrambled over the boulder and crashed through some thick shrubs, disappearing from sight. The motorcycle cops squealed to a stop. Their headlamps illuminated the boulder and foliage behind it.

"What's back there?" one of the cops shouted to the other.

"The zoo," his partner answered.

"Good. We've got him now. Let's go."

They revved their engines and roared off. They raced through the zoo, prowling the network of pathways and finally stopped outside the lion's habitat. They climbed off their motorcycles and drew their guns.

"This is where he would have entered," one of the cops said.

"Right into the lion's den," the other cop said. "You think he's still in there?"

"I don't know. Maybe. The big cats are probably asleep."

They shone their flashlights into the habitat, and one of the lions leaped up directly in front of them and roared. Its fangs flashed in the light, and its claws ripped at the protective fencing. The cops jumped back.

"He sure as heck isn't around here," one of them said. "Let's keep looking."

"Good, boy," the Phantom said, and petted the lion's head as the cops hurried away. Then he scaled the fence, but he didn't make it over quite in time.

"There he is!" one of the cops yelled, and chased him on foot.

The Phantom dashed out of the zoo and down one of the park's paved roads. Suddenly a car appeared in the Phantom's path, its bright lights shining in his eyes. He dodged off the road as the car screeched to a halt.

"Get in!" a familiar voice yelled.

The Phantom looked past the blinding lights. It

was Al, the cabby! He was only half into the vehicle when Al squealed away, leaving behind the cops, who were now separated from their motorcycles.

Diana glanced through the back window of the car, past the motorcycle escort. She was sure that, for a moment, she had seen the Phantom on horseback trailing after them. But now there was no sign of him. And she still didn't know what had happened to Kit Walker.

"Turn around," ordered Drax, who was sitting next to her. "Forget about him. He's not coming along on this little trip."

Sala turned around from the front seat, and smiled. "He's probably dead by now."

"What's wrong with you?" Diana demanded.

"I could ask you the same thing, you know."

"You're mean," Diana snapped, heat rising in her voice. "You don't care about anything or anyone."

"Like what? Tell me what I should care about and I'll give it some thought."

"You figure it out," Diana shot back.

Drax's irritation had reached monumental proportions. He slammed his fist against the dashboard. "That's enough. Everyone shut up and enjoy the ride."

Sala turned her face toward the window. From the back where Diana was, she could see that the other woman was distressed. Diana wondered if she had hit a nerve.

"You've got to find that Pierce-Arrow, Al," the Phantom said. "They're probably heading to the airport."

The cabby shook his head. "Drax is heading for the docks. I picked it up on my police band. Thought you and Kit would want to know."

"Thanks. Step on it."

The cabby accelerated out of the park and into traffic, dodging between cars. The Phantom sat back and realized, suddenly, that he wasn't the only passenger.

"Dad?"

"Don't get so comfortable. It's the bottom of the ninth and you're two skulls behind."

"I know. I know. I'm doing all I can."

The cabby glanced curiously into his rearview mirror. Then he shrugged, assuming that the Phantom was talking to himself.

"Dad, a man named Quill has a gun belt like the one I wear. Is it yours?"

"Does he smoke cigars?" his father asked.

"That's him."

"He told me he could take me to the stronghold of the Sengh Brotherhood," his ghostly father confided. "I trusted him. He led me to a place deep in the jungle. It was a trick. He stabbed me in the back. Literally."

The Phantom stared at him in disbelief. He had idolized his father, had thought that he was infallible. No one could fool him.

"So sue me," his father said. "I was a lousy judge of character."

"I'm going to get that gun belt back. That's a promise. Besides, I owe Quill a few myself."

"If you haven't lost them by now."

"I'll catch them. I have to." He looked over at his father again. "There's a woman involved."

"Well, saints be praised. It's about time." His father motioned toward the driver. "Tell him to step on it. Your trip to the zoo didn't help matters."

The Phantom leaned forward. "Can you go any faster?"

The cabby looked into the rearview mirror. "You talking to me now?"

"Yes. Can you pick it up?"

"Sure. Hold on to your hat . . . or, whatever."

The Phantom turned back to his father. "I didn't see you at the zoo." But the seat was empty.

Ten minutes later, the taxi screeched to a stop at Pier 39 at the New York Harbor. The motorcycle patrol was just pulling away. The Phantom jumped out and spotted Drax and the others boarding a small seaplane.

"It looks like I have a plane to catch."

"Give my best to Mr. Walker," the cabby yelled after him. But the Phantom was already racing along the pier. He dove into the harbor and began swimming.

"I love New York," the cabby said as he drove off.

The Phantom's arms chopped through the chilly waters, and he kicked his legs as fast as he could. He was moving so swiftly that his torso was nearly planing across the surface of the water. He was making steady progress, but he was still twenty-five yards away from the seaplane when its engine revved to life.

He tried to swim faster, taking longer and longer strokes, and kicking harder. Almost there.

But with less than ten yards to go, the plane started

to taxi away. He kept swimming madly after it, but it was no use. He'd arrived at the pier a minute too late.

He was treading water, a gusty wind whipped his face. The plane gained speed as his hopes fell. Then to his surprise it turned and taxied in the opposite direction—straight toward him. The pilot probably wanted to take advantage of the tailwind.

He ducked under the surface and swam toward the plane. He came up for air once and judged the distance between himself and the plane and the speed that the plane was moving. He ducked under again. As the Phantom swam, the whine of the engine grew louder. He kicked hard and exploded out of the water. He reached up just as the plane was lifting off the water and grabbed the pontoon with both hands.

For a moment, he thought his arms were going to be jerked out of their sockets by the accelerating plane. Then he managed to wrap his legs around the pontoon. Finally, as the plane rose above the harbor, he crawled around the pontoon until he was perched on top of it.

He leaned forward, hugging the pontoon to limit the wind resistance. "It's going to be a long night," he told himself.

TWENTY-FIVE

The night of flight, far longer than only the Phantom could have imagined, was finally coming to an end. Drax was in the cockpit, with Sala watching, as the night slowly faded into a steel-gray haze. He had been too excited to sleep. Maybe he'd never sleep again. Once he had the third skull in his possession, anything, absolutely anything, was possible.

He chuckled to himself. If ol' David Palmer thought his influence was widespread now, just wait. Without a doubt, Drax knew he would be the single-most powerful person in the world. No statesman, no general, no president, no dictator would ever come close to the type of power he would possess. With a single command, he would be able to destroy nations, bury continents, even destroy the world itself when he was ready to move on to other worlds. Yes, truly anything was possible.

Even his mother would be proud of him, if she were still alive. She'd raised him by herself, in poverty, and she'd always told him to do whatever he could to be the greatest person he could be, and not to let anyone stop him.

That was exactly what he'd done, too, and he'd

done it for her. He always tried to make up for his shortcomings. If he hadn't been late coming home that night when he was eighteen, his mother would still be alive. She'd left a candle burning for him as she always did. The cat had probably knocked it over and the curtains had caught fire. The house had burned and taken her life.

"Almost dawn," Sala said wearily. "We should be near the island. If there is one."

"Don't start doubting me now," Drax said as he consulted the map, and checked their bearings. "We're getting very close now."

"Look! What's that?" Sala pointed out the window to a dark mass protruding from the cloud cover.

"A volcano. That's it!" Drax shouted. "There *is* an island! Go down! We found it."

Sala took a deep breath, then pulled back on the throttle. The plane began a steep descent.

Rejoicing, vindicated, Drax turned in his seat and woke up the others to tell them the news. "Get ready! We're landing!"

They dipped down into a thick blanket of fog. "I can't see a thing," Sala said, sounding worried as the seaplane continued its descent.

"Don't worry. You're doing just fine. Keep going," Drax urged. "Keep going."

Quill, Zephro, and Diana were now awake, but they didn't seem to be sharing Drax's early morning enthusiasm.

Suddenly the fog parted. And just in time. Choppy waters loomed just below them. Sala pulled back on the yoke. The plane leveled and skimmed across the water a couple of hundred yards from shore.

"We made it!" Zephro shouted, sounding relieved.

"No time to waste," Drax said, looking out toward the rocky shoreline. "Inflate the raft. Grab the supplies. We've got work to do."

A few minutes later, the seaplane was anchored, and the life raft inflated. They climbed down onto the pontoon and into the raft. Quill manned a pair of oars, while Sala, Zephro, and Diana squeezed into the center of the raft. Drax, meanwhile, played George Washington crossing the Delaware as he stood at the bow with one foot raised on the rim of the raft. He gazed with steadfast concentration toward the rocky shore.

Resting in the bottom of the raft, just behind him, was the leather satchel containing the two Skulls of Touganda. He knew he was taking a chance traveling with the skulls, but he wanted the three skulls joined together as quickly as possible.

"Yes, I see an opening, a cave. Let's go take a look. Straight ahead, Quill."

It wasn't long before they picked up speed as the surf washed them toward shore. "More to the port side," Drax yelled as they bobbed on the rising and falling sea.

Drax remained at his post unaffected by the choppy sea, but everyone else looked nauseous and frightened, especially Charlie Zephro. "Hang on, almost there," Drax said encouragingly.

Then a large wave rolled in and swept them toward the rocky cliff. Drax wobbled and lost his balance. He grabbed a rope handle to keep from being tossed over the side.

"Oh, no!" Zephro yelled. "We're going to hit the rocks."

"Paddle!" Drax yelled at Quill, who was struggling to keep the raft from spinning into pinnacles of rock, which jutted menacingly through the surf.

Just when it looked as if the raft were about to be ripped to shreds, they were washed swiftly to the left and into the cave. They drifted with the current into the opening. The waters were dark and smooth. They seemed to glide over the surface.

As Drax's eyes adjusted to the dim light, he saw that they were winding between the banks of what looked like a European coastal village made of quaint stone buildings, bordered by stone walls and stairways.

"What is this place?" Sala asked.

No one had an answer. They all stared in wonder.

"It's an underground village," Diana finally offered.

"Are we going to stop?" Zephro asked.

"There doesn't seem to be anyone here," Quill said. "It's totally deserted."

Finally Drax spoke up. "We're so close now that I can feel it! History is about to be made, and you're all a part of it." He paused, considering the implications of what he'd just said. "Not an equal part, of course, but an important part, nonetheless."

They drifted beneath an arched bridge, and suddenly men were leaping over the side, landing in the hip-deep water. The raft was quickly surrounded as Sala let out a startled scream.

In another part of the village, the Phantom heard the scream. He drew his pistols and moved hastily toward it. The streets were empty, but he didn't think the village was deserted. Its condition was too good. There were no fallen walls, no signs of the inevitable decay that results from abandonment.

He tried to stay alert, but he wasn't in the best condition after spending the night on the pontoon. He'd managed to wedge himself under a strut, and he'd actually fallen asleep a few times, but only briefly. The wind had been cold and constant, penetrating his clothing, numbing his fingers.

But he'd been fast asleep when the plane started its descent and, if not for the strut, he would've been tossed off the pontoon. As they dove through the chilly mist, he had no idea where they were or what was below them. Then he smelled the sea air, and a moment later the curtain of fog opened and the waters appeared. As soon as the plane touched down, he slipped off the pontoon and into the relatively warm waters.

He'd spotted the cavern and swam toward it, loosening up his aching body. After a few hundred feet, he paused to watch Drax and the others launch an inflatable raft. He was interested in exploring the cavern, but he wanted to make sure that Drax had the same idea.

After a few minutes, the rafters passed within ten yards of him as he sank below the surface. Then he followed them toward the cavern. He saw how the waves were pushing the raft into the rocks, so he compensated by swimming hard in the opposite direction. He arrived at the cavern entrance a couple minutes behind the rafters.

Now he hurried through the village and ducked down behind a wall when the bridge crossing the channel came into view. Several armed men were walking away with the rafters. To the Phantom's surprise, no one—not even Quill or Sala or Zephro—were struggling to get away. They seemed to go voluntarily.

There was something familiar about the captors, familiar and loathsome. Then he noticed a design carved into the rock wall of the cavern, a large spider web, the emblem of the Sengh Brotherhood. So, he'd finally found their hideout, or at least one of them.

The sudden attack took Diana by surprise as much as the others. They were quickly surrounded by guns and sabers and pulled out of the raft. A huge, ugly thug with a battered nose, a ragged scar on his cheek, and a permanent snarl ran a hand over her body and leered at her with his one good eye. He wore tattered clothes and a kerchief on his head. She pulled back from him and, as she did, noticed a spider-web tattoo on his forearm.

"This one is mine," he growled. "All mine."

"Not in your dreams," Diana shot back.

Ugly Mug grabbed her with both hands, and instantly Sala sprang forward. She spun Ugly Mug around and kicked him hard in the groin. A second pirate leaped forward and grabbed Sala. Diana returned the favor by slugging the thug and knocking him out cold with a solid right hook. The other attackers raised their sabers and aimed their pistols.

Quill shouted, "Take it easy, my brothers! Stay calm!"

"Brothers?" A burly, bald-headed pirate wearing a dirty kerchief around his neck stepped forward. "What do you mean? Why do you call us brothers?"

Quill pushed up his sleeve, revealing the spider-web tattoo on his forearm. "We are also members of the Sengh Brotherhood."

The bald pirate turned and huddled with the others, who kept glancing their way, weapons still raised.

"Nice going," Drax murmured to Quill.

Diana realized that although Drax might be knowledgeable about the Sengh Brotherhood, he didn't know all of their secrets. The village was as much of a surprise to him as it had been to her, and his so-called brothers had nearly killed him.

But now, thanks to Quill's quick thinking, the tension had eased. The bald pirate motioned to them. "Come with us."

As the group moved off, Diana and Sala straightened their clothes and pushed back their hair. "Good show back there, girl," Sala said, taking Diana by the arm. "I think we'd better stick together."

Diana glanced back and saw that Ugly Mug was lurking just behind her. Better to deal with Sala, she thought, than with the thug behind her. "Good idea," she replied, and hurried ahead.

They walked out of the village, hiked over a mound of loose rocks, and moved toward the wall. There, they climbed over a rock outcropping and stepped into a dark tunnel, its entrance hidden from view. Diana had the feeling she wasn't going to like this place, and as soon as she was inside, she knew it.

The air smelled like dirty socks. The walls and floors were wet and slippery. They moved along a winding passageway that descended a gentle slope. Squealing rats ran under foot and huge spiders guarded their webs. But what really made her squeamish was the sight of human skeletons, dozens of them, chained to the walls in horribly contorted positions. Not a few had broken bones. These people had not died well.

She wondered how many years they had remained there, reminders of the penalty for misdeeds against the Brotherhood. Or maybe for just being in the wrong place at the wrong time. That was exactly the situation in which she found herself.

Then they passed under a high stone arch and entered an immense chamber. Several large masts, cocked at odd angles, reached up toward the high ceiling. Riggings and unfurled sails hung overhead. Spread out in piles throughout the chamber was the booty plundered from ships and villages. The flags of looted ships were displayed from a yardarm. It was like a trophy room, she thought.

Diana took it all in as she and the others crossed a bridge over a moat. She glanced down into the dark waters, where sharks cruised under the bridge, their fins visible just above the surface of the water.

She had the distinct feeling that the sharks had tasted human flesh, maybe had even developed a preference for it.

At the far end of the enormous chamber, a figure was seated on a wooden throne, which was raised on a platform that resembled a ship's poop deck. As they moved closer to the man, Diana saw a large banner on the wall behind the throne that displayed the spider-web symbol.

The guards stopped them several yards from the throne, and Diana turned her attention to the man gazing down at them. He had thin lips and piercing dark eyes. He was at least sixty with short gray hair, and he appeared to be of Euro-Asian descent.

He was dressed in a loose-fitting black silk outfit. He wore a short goatee and a gold medallion bearing the spider-web insignia around his neck. His face showed no emotion. He looked neither pleased nor angry at their arrival, but his gaze sent cold licks along her spine.

All around him were relics, no doubt his favorite booty, and prominent among them was a life-sized gold skull, which rested on a pedestal within his reach. Without a doubt, Diana thought, it was the third skull of Touganda, the treasured artifact of power. She glanced at Drax and saw that he couldn't take his eyes off the glimmering skull. If he knew the man seated on the throne, he gave no indication of it.

"Visitors!" the man said, stroking his chin. "Now let me see, how long has it been since we've had visitors down here, thirty fathoms beneath the ocean's surface . . . in the bowels of this uncharted volcanic island?"

A beat passed before he answered his own question. "Never! Congratulations! You pathetic doomed fools are the first."

TWENTY-SIX

The laughter of the man on the throne echoed through the chamber as the Phantom darted across the bridge unnoticed. He moved ahead, skulking from one pile of loot to another.

These guys needed a housekeeper, he thought. The place was in more disarray than his Treasure Chamber. There was also a lot of junk mixed in with the loot, broken chairs and tables, pieces of steamer trunks and boats, even a rusted airplane propeller.

When he was within a hundred feet of the throne, he ducked behind a pile of rope at the base of a rigging that reached the ceiling. The Sengh Brotherhood banner stretched across a wall behind the throne. Now he knew for certain that he had finally found their stronghold.

He wanted to get a closer vantage point and remain out of view, so he carefully climbed a rigging. When he was near the top, he leaped onto a ledge thirty feet above the floor. He crept forward until he was directly to the side of the throne, which was twenty feet below him. He crouched down in the shadows beyond the illumination of the torches. He could see and hear everything, but was invisible, he believed, to the pirates and their captives.

Ever since one of his ancestors had destroyed the Sengh castle on Bangalla, the line of Phantoms had hunted for the new headquarters. But they had never come to this part of the world. There was something here that had served to protect the Brotherhood over the centuries, and now the Phantom knew what it was. The gold skull.

It glinted in the light of the torches and seemed to possess an illumination of its own. It had the same strange, alien beauty as the other two skulls, the Phantom thought, and mesmerized him.

"Congratulations, Kit." His father was suddenly sitting on the ledge next to him. "You've hit the mother lode! You've found the secret hideout of the Sengh Brotherhood."

He nodded and spoke softly. "I figured as much."

His father was elated. "I could hug you, my boy," and he did exactly that, his ghostly arms wrapping around the Phantom's shoulders as though they were solid. It was an eerie sensation and yet firm enough to seem real.

The elder Walker peered down into the chamber, taking in the entire scene. His tone shifted now from elation to concern. "You're outnumbered, son."

Like he hadn't already figured that out.

Sometimes, Kit thought, his father was more annoying than he was helpful. The Phantom focused his attention on the man who occupied the throne, the nefarious leader of the Brotherhood.

It had been a long time since the two of them had seen each other. But as far as the Phantom was concerned, it wasn't long enough. He despised the man so deeply he couldn't even bring himself to utter his name aloud.

He watched as his nemesis motioned to the bald pirate. "Who are these people?"

Before the pirate could speak, Drax stepped forward. "My name is Xander Drax."

He'd decided the best way of dealing with this little despot was to play his game. Give him some respect, as if he was actually impressed. Make him think that he, Drax, felt subservient to his highness on the wooden throne.

"What?"

Obviously this fellow didn't keep up on current affairs in America or he would've reacted in a little less ignorant manner. "X-A-N-D-E-R D-R-A-X," he said, spelling it out. Not that it would help if this tyrant was as illiterate as Drax suspected. "Xander Drax. Begins and ends with the letter X." He raised his chin. "From New York City. And you, sir . . . as long as we're making introductions and polite chit-chat—"

"He's the Great Kabai Sengh!" snapped the big, bald pirate. "The supreme leader of the Sengh."

"Direct descendant of the Evil Kabai Sengh, the first leader of the Sengh Brotherhood," Sengh added.

Diana leaned toward Sala. "If this guy's the great one, imagine what the evil one was like."

Drax turned to Quill. "So, you weren't kidding, these guys are really around. How do you like that?"

"Stop the whispering!" Sengh commanded. "You're a long way from New York. How did you find this place?"

"I'll show you," Drax said.

For the grand finale, he would zing old Sengh. He set his satchel on the floor, and as he reached inside of it, two pirates raised their weapons. But Kabai Sengh motioned them to lower their pistols when Drax lifted out two skulls, one in each hand.

Holding them up for inspection, ''These skulls brought me here,'' he declared. ''The Skulls of Touganda!''

Sengh looked genuinely startled. ''How do you know of such matters?'' he hissed.

''Oh, I know all about these skulls.'' Let him mull that one over. ''And the powers they contain—once all three are united: the two I hold, and the one you have there.''

Kabai Sengh glanced at his gold skull. ''I am the one who will bring them together.''

Drax took another step closer to Sengh. It was time to straighten the old fellow out. Sengh was far from frail, but he wasn't exactly robust, either. Drax guessed he could overcome the Sengh leader and use him as a hostage to get his way. But he hoped it wouldn't come to that. He preferred negotiation to strong-arm tactics, at least as long as the negotiations were working in his favor.

''Look, Great One. I really wasn't in the market for a partner, but it seems to me we have a mutually beneficial situation here.''

He paused to let Sengh consider his words before he continued. ''Think of it this way: you represent the old guard of the grizzled scalawags and Peg-Leg Petes, while I stand for the new order of things— modern and up to date. Just the man to carry our cause onward into the twentieth century.''

''Silence! You have no bargaining power with me,

Mr. New York City! I could kill you, all of you, right now, and feed your pretty pink carcasses to the sharks!''

Drax realized that negotiations weren't going to work. He needed to take Sengh hostage, and fast. But before he could act, Sengh threw him off balance with a single comment. ''Besides, Mr. Drax, you don't have the fourth skull.''

''The fourth skull? What fourth skull? What are you talking about? There is no fourth skull.''

''Yes, there is,'' Sengh replied, and smiled for the first time since they'd entered the stronghold.

The Phantom leaned forward so far he nearly fell off the ledge. Perplexed by this new development, he turned to his father and whispered, ''Dad, what do you know about this fourth skull?''

He shrugged. ''It's news to me.''

It was a trick, Drax thought. ''No, there's not. There can't be. I've studied it.''

''And I've lived it.'' He crossed his arms. ''Burned ships and villages. Plunged my saber into flesh and bone. Bathed in the blood of my victims. Feasted on their pain and misery. Danced to their screams of agony.'' He grinned, his filthy teeth lining up in his mouth like a stained picket fence. ''And I've relished every minute of it.''

Drax glanced at Zephro. ''What a bunch of phony pirate crap.''

''Trust me,'' Sengh said. ''The fourth skull controls the power of the three. Without it, you have wasted your time . . . and your lives.''

Sengh signaled his men to dispatch the captives.

Guns and sabers were suddenly pointed at them as if the men lived to spill blood.

"Wait a minute!" Drax shouted. Once again, he was ready to negotiate. "If anything happens to us, others will come looking. They know where we are. You'll have an entire army down your throat. Think about that before you slaughter us."

But Charlie Zephro had other ideas. He pulled a pistol from an ankle holster and aimed it at Kabai Sengh. "That's a lie. Nobody knows where we are."

"What're you doing?" Drax shouted.

"Shut up! Spirit of adventure, ha! It's every man for himself now." He turned to Sengh. "Okay, Kabai, now it's time to sing a different tune. Get me outta here or you *really* sleep with the fishes. What have you got to say about that?"

Sengh reacted calmly. *"Shin nebo."*

"What's that supposed to mean?" Zephro asked.

"Oh, it's just ancient pirate talk for . . . 'fire the cannon.' "

Zephro looked around. "Huh?"

Suddenly he realized that a cannon was pointed directly at him, and the fuse was lit.

As large as the cavern was, the sound of well-wadded and packed gunpowder exploding filled it easily, rippling the stolen standards and even bending the crooked masts.

The small cannon ball whistled through the air and hit Charlie squarely in the gut. The impact was so powerful, he was knocked all the way to the wall, where he crumpled like a lowered flag.

"You see what I mean, Mr. Drax, about your bargaining power here?" Sengh said.

For once, Drax didn't know what to say.

*   *   *

The blast of the cannon must have caused something to click inside the Phantom's head. He snapped his fingers. "Dad, I know where the fourth skull is."

"You do? Where?"

He didn't answer. Instead he leaped from his hiding place to the rigging and climbed out over the floor of the chamber.

Diana was stunned by the swift justice Sengh had served upon Zephro. Never mind that the thug deserved whatever was coming to him. Never mind that at all. The point was that whatever plea she might put forward about her own case—that she was a captive herself and had nothing whatsoever to do with this plot—wouldn't make a difference.

Sengh couldn't care less about who or what she was. Drawing attention to herself would end her life as suddenly as it had ended Zephro's.

But Quill had other ideas. "I am Quill, Great Kabai Sengh. A loyal follower and soldier. Look . . ." He pointed to his belt. "I killed the Phantom."

"You killed the Phantom?" Sengh said.

"Yes, Kabai Sengh."

He laughed. "Well, join the club. Many of us have killed the Phantom over the years. But he just doesn't go away!"

Diana looked up and saw the Phantom climbing in the rigging directly overhead. "You can say that again," she murmured. Sala, who was standing next to her, followed her gaze. The Phantom motioned for them to remain quiet.

The two women glanced at each other in astonishment, then Sala pointed at the floor. "Oh, Diana, you dropped your pearl necklace there on the floor."

Diana realized that Sala was attempting to divert the attention of anyone who might have noticed them looking up. She immediately dropped to one knee, scooped a hand through the shadows, then adjusted the necklace on her throat. "Thanks. I didn't realize I'd dropped it."

Quill shook his head. "I can't believe that's all you're worried about."

"What do you know?" Sala snapped.

"More than you'll ever figure out," Quill snapped back.

"Shut up, both of you," Drax said.

Sala glared at him. "Don't tell me to shut up, you arrogant bully."

Drax just smiled and said, "Hey, Kabai, I can see this Phantom thing really strikes a nerve. In that case, you're gonna love this." He pointed at Diana. "She's his girlfriend."

"Great," Diana muttered.

"Bring her here!" Sengh ordered.

TWENTY-SEVEN

Diana struggled as several pirates dragged her forward to Kabai Sengh. She didn't like being used as a bargaining tool. Nor did she like the way Sengh eyed her, as though she would soon be another trophy to have on his throne.

"Think of the opportunities this presents, Kabai Sengh," Drax boasted. "Ransom . . . bait . . . revenge. It's wonderful."

Diana glared at him. *Yes, just wonderful,* she thought. She didn't know which of the two men she despised more—Drax or Sengh.

"The Phantom's got good taste," Sengh said, looking her over.

"Ah, good! I overlooked that one—personal pleasure!" Drax nodded, approving Sengh's lusty thoughts. "So, waddaya say, Kabai Sengh? The girl for the skull and I'm outta your hair."

Sengh reached out to touch Diana's face, but she slapped his hand, pushing him away. "You pirates need to get out more."

Enraged by her rejection, he leaped to his feet and drew a saber from beside the throne. For a moment, she was sure he intended to cut her head off. But he was interrupted by a shout from above.

"Kabai Sengh!" hollered the Phantom from the top of the mast.

Sengh's head dropped back. "Phantom!" Sengh grunted.

"Fancy seeing you here, Sengh."

The Phantom grabbed a rope, swung down from the mast, and collided with Sengh, who tumbled off the platform. Pandemonium erupted and the pirates rushed to the throne, shouting and waving their swords. The Phantom pulled out both of his pistols and fired at the attackers. Sabers and guns flew from the hands of several, while many others hit the floor.

One pirate grabbed him around the neck from behind. The Phantom jammed his elbow back hard, smashing the assailant in the nose. Another one lunged at him and the Phantom introduced his jaw to the butt of his pistol. Both men slumped to the floor, unconscious.

Amid the uproar, Drax was moving stealthily toward the gold skull. Holstering his pistols, the Phantom darted over to it and scooped it away from him. At the same moment, a pirate took a swing at the Phantom, who ducked, and the punch struck Drax.

Kabai Sengh was back on his feet. He charged the Phantom, brandishing his saber, waving it through the air. "Ghost Who Walks, huh? I'll cut you off at the knees! You won't be walking after that!"

The Phantom leaped to avoid the low first slash, then ducked just in time to keep his head from parting with the rest of his body. He ducked and jumped a few more times as he backed away from the throne, grabbing a discarded belaying pin as he did. He used it to fend of one blow after another, until he had retreated to the edge of the moat. Just behind him, he could hear the excited sharks slapping the water with their fins. One more step and he was dinner.

"You're not immortal! I know your secrets, Phantom!" Sengh bellowed.

As he spoke, Sengh lunged at the Phantom with his most forceful blow. The Phantom deftly side-stepped the thrust and brought the belaying pin down on the back of Sengh's neck. Sengh screamed as he plunged into the moat.

"Take them to your grave, Kabai Sengh," the Phantom said as the sharks attacked the floundering pirate king.

But the Phantom had made a mistake by turning his back to the rest of the pirates. Suddenly several of them rushed at him at once, their weapons raised.

Diana knew the Phantom was in trouble. She had to do something to help him, and she had to do it quickly. Then she saw the possibility, glimpsed it hanging just above them. She picked up a sword from the floor.

"Sala! Catch!"

Sala turned to Diana just as she tossed the sword to her. She snatched it above her head.

"Cut that rope!" Diana yelled, pointing to a taut rope anchored to the floor.

Sala turned to her right, and without a moment's hesitation, she slashed through it. A rope net dropped down, ensnaring the charging pirates just before they reached the Phantom. The net was fixed to a pulley, and before the pirates could free themselves, they were hoisted up into the rigging high overhead.

"Thanks," the Phantom said. "I thought I was going to have my hands full there."

"Don't mention it," Diana responded. "Sala did the hard part."

"That net won't hold them long," the Phantom said, glancing up. "We've got to get out of here."

"Take me with you," Sala pleaded. "I'm not one of these brotherhood guys."

The Phantom hesitated, no doubt wondering if she could be trusted.

"She's basically a good kid," Diana said. She'd actually grown to like Sala.

That was enough for the Phantom. "This way."

They rushed across the chamber, over a bridge, and through a dark passageway. After a few yards, the passageway forked.

The Phantom stopped. "Great. Which one did you take to get here?"

Diana looked at Sala, who shrugged. "It's hard to say. They look the same."

"Yeah, they do, but I've got the feeling they don't lead to the same place."

Sala glanced around uneasily. "We'd better not wait around or it won't matter which one we take."

The Phantom pointed to one, then the other, then the first one, and finally back to the other. "Okay. Let's go this way."

They raced down the passageway to the left. It twisted, dropped, and rose. Diana realized this passage was cleaner and drier than the one they'd been in earlier. There were no rats or spiders, and no skeletons.

"I'm not sure this is the right way," she said.

"It's too late to go back now," the Phantom said. "Besides, this might be a better way out."

They rushed along the curving wall and suddenly the passageway came to an abrupt end at an iron door. The Phantom tested the handle. Locked. He took out one of his pistols. "Step back!"

He fired twice at the lock, tried the door again. It was still locked or stuck. He kicked it, rammed it with his shoulder, but it wouldn't give. He tried again with the same result.

"Hold it," Diana said. She'd noticed a button on the wall to the right of the door. She pressed it and heard a faint buzzing sound. "Try it now."

This time the Phantom turned the knob and the door swung open. "Good going," he said. "Let's just hope the buzzer didn't give us away."

As soon as they stepped into the room, they forgot about their concern. The walls and ceiling were made of iron, and several huge bullet-shaped cannisters were stacked near a couple of firing tubes. They didn't look like they were there as conversation pieces, either. On one wall was a control panel; a periscope hung from the ceiling. It looked like something out of a Jules Verne novel, Diana thought.

"Torpedoes!" The Phantom was fascinated.

Diana immediately realized the implications. "I bet this just might explain all those missing ships in the Devil's Vortex."

"Could be," the Phantom said, but his thoughts were elsewhere. He looked over one of the torpedoes, then slid back a panel to reveal a long hollow section inside. "You and Sala can escape inside here. I'll shoot you to the surface."

"What?" Sala exclaimed. "That's nuts." She stabbed a thumb at the torpedo. "There's a live warhead on there. If it hits anything, we're fish food."

"It won't hit anything," the Phantom assured her. "I'll use the periscope to make sure the path is clear."

"What about you?" Diana asked. "How will you get out of here?"

The Phantom looked around the room. "Don't worry about me. I'll be right behind you."

"But how?" Diana asked.

"No time to explain. C'mon. Climb in. It's time for a ride."

Diana stepped into the torpedo, but suddenly she wasn't so sure about it. "What about air, Phantom? How are we going to breathe?"

"You'll have enough to last."

"We'll make it," Sala said. "The Phantom's right. We better hurry."

They both squeezed into the torpedo, and the Phantom slid the panel shut. The darkness closed in around them, thick and crippling. Claustrophobia clutched at her, nearly suffocated her. She forced herself to take several deep, calming breaths. It helped, but deep breaths weren't going to get her to the surface without her losing her mind.

She hoped it wasn't going to take long for the Phantom to launch the torpedo.

The Phantom hurried over to a spool of thick chain that was attached to a winch. He hooked the end of the chain to the back of the torpedo and jerked on it, testing its strength.

He was fairly certain it was strong enough to pull

him to the surface. Like he'd told Diana, he would be right behind them.

He moved over to the periscope and peered through the eyepiece. The path was clear. There was no ship visible anywhere nearby. Next he studied the control panel. He pulled back on a lever and the torpedo was immediately loaded into the firing tube.

"Good. Almost ready," he said to himself.

He froze in place, sensing that he wasn't alone in the room. "Dad?"

No answer.

He whirled around, a punch clipped his jaw. A very human blow. The Phantom stumbled back against a wall, and the gold skull fell from his grasp. Quill grinned and brandished a knife as the skull clattered across the metal floor.

It stopped right in front of Drax, who was holding the satchel with the other two skulls tightly to his chest.

TWENTY-EIGHT

Quill lunged at the Phantom, driving the knife toward his heart. But the Phantom twisted to the side and the blade merely scraped his purple jerkin. The Phantom grabbed his wrist. They struggled for the knife, their faces just inches apart.

"I killed you ten years ago!" Quill growled through his gritted teeth.

"No, you idiot, you killed my father!" The Phantom twisted his wrist, the knife dropped to the floor, he kicked it aside and dove for Quill's legs. They crashed to the floor together.

They each threw one punch after another, arms flying like pistons. They rolled, slammed into a wall, rolled again. Quill wrapped his hands around the Phantom's throat and squeezed until stars literally exploded in the Phantom's eyes. He jackknifed the lower part of his body, his knee slamming into Quill's groin, and Quill's hands loosened enough for the Phantom to suck in air and toss him off.

He scrambled to his feet, spun, and kicked Quill in the ribs. Quill doubled over, groaning and clutching himself, then sprang up like a huge, agile cat and slammed into the Phantom. They fell again, rolled, each struggling to gain the advantage. It seemed to the Phantom like a kind of hell, an endless loop that he couldn't escape.

Drax was oblivious to the life-and-death struggle between the two men. His gaze was fixed on the gold skull at his feet, and his eyes glistened as he bent down and picked it up. Now he had the three skulls.

"At last . . ." His voice was barely more than a whisper. His hands were shaking.

Suddenly the silver and jade skulls flew from the satchel, propelled by their own power, and the gold skull turned hot as coals in his hands. He let go of the skull and it leaped into the air with the other two, locking together in the shape of a pyramid. The eyes of the skulls began to glow, the pounding of drums filled the room, and the temperature plunged.

Blood rushed out of Drax's face and he backed away, enthralled but terrified that the surge of energy, when it came, would overpower him.

"What's taking so long?" Diana was hot, cramped, and finding it more and more difficult to breathe.

"I don't know," Sala answered. "Something must have gone wrong."

"Let's try to get out of here. The Phantom must need our help," Diana said.

"We need help," Sala responded. "The panel is locked. I can't move it."

"What's that?" Diana asked. "Do you hear it?"

The drumming reverberated around them, shaking the torpedo. "Maybe we're on our way!" Sala said hopefully.

But Diana had heard the same pounding beat in the museum when Drax had united the silver and jade skulls. She didn't know what it meant, but she didn't like it. The thought of dying in this tin can sent a ripple of chills through her. Her hands curled into fists. She couldn't think of a more horrible way to die. But she would go insane before she suffocated. She was sure that she was already starting to lose her mind.

She tried to pound on the wall of the torpedo, but there wasn't enough space. Besides, with the drumming, nobody would hear it anyhow. She squeezed her eyes shut. Trapped.

They were on their feet now, locked together, spinning, when the Phantom was slammed into the control panel. Quill pulled him away, then shoved him into the panel again. This time the Phantom felt a lever move. He heard a roaring sound through the incessant drumming and realized that he'd just fired the torpedo. It shot out of its tube, and the chain attached to the torpedo began to rapidly unwind.

The Phantom twisted around, pushed Quill against the wall, and pressed his forearms into his throat. Quill gagged and gasped for air; the skull tattoos on his cheeks burned bright red.

"You have something that belongs to me," the Phantom shouted over the din of the drums. His free hand moved down toward Quill's waist. He snatched the skull-head gun belt, ripped it loose, and hooked it inside his own belt.

This was Destiny with a capital *D;* his Destiny. There was no turning back now. The future of the skulls and Drax's life were intricately entwined. The power was there, and it was his.

He reached up and grabbed the pyramid of floating skulls with both hands. His fingers slipped into convenient holes between the skulls that seemed made for just this purpose.

Bolts of blue light shot from the jewel-encrusted eye sockets of the three skulls. They converged to form a ray of light so bright that Drax couldn't look at it for more than a second. He smelled melting iron and saw that the ray had burned a huge hole in the iron-plated wall.

Holding the skulls tightly, he turned and beamed the ray toward the Phantom. But the Phantom, who was still fighting with Quill, turned around and jerked Quill in front of him.

Quill was instantly vaporized. One moment the Phantom had held his shoulder, the next he was gone. Not a trace of him remained behind. Then the ray faded and disappeared.

Drax circled one way, the Phantom the other. What happened to the ray? Drax wondered. How could he get it started again? Then he smiled as the skulls glowed, energizing themselves.

"The skulls are more powerful than I ever imagined," Drax gloated. "You haven't seen anything yet. I've harnessed the energy of the sun. Who needs a fourth skull, if there even is one?"

The Phantom glanced from Drax toward the unspooling chain, then back to Drax again. "There is a fourth skull, and I know where it is," the Phantom said.

"That's a lie."

"I've worn it all my life . . . for protection," the Phantom said. "But I've never understood what that meant until now."

"We'll see about that!" Drax raised the skulls and they discharged a full blast of their blue death. At the same moment, the Phantom lifted his fist and the death rays converged directly on his skull ring.

For a moment, the ring held the incredible flow of energy in check, then reflected it back toward the three skulls. But the legendary skulls continued to pour out their lethal blue light.

The Phantom used every ounce of strength at his command to repel the death ray. He held his outstretched fist in place with his other hand, but he slowly sank to one knee. He grimaced in pain, sweat streamed profusely down his forehead.

"Die, die, die!" shouted Drax.

The struggle was grueling. It sapped his strength, bit by painful bit, until he didn't know how much longer he would last. With a final effort, he drew on reserves he didn't realize he had and pushed his fist and the skull ring a couple of inches closer to Drax and the three skulls.

He felt as-if he were on fire, as if he were about to be vaporized. Then the skulls, overcome with their own reflected power, exploded in a flash of brilliant light. The Phantom covered his eyes with his arm but kept his ring hand extended. When he finally lowered it, the skulls were gone.

And so was Drax.

At that moment, the spool of chain ran out. It pulled tight on the drum, snapped, and the Phantom dove for it. He grabbed the end of the chain and shot through the firing tube and into the sea.

As the torpedo sliced through the murky depths, the Phantom began working his way up the chain, hand over fist, fighting the enormous opposing force of the water crushing against him. As a kid, he used to practice holding his breath under water, and he'd been able to exceed three minutes. But he'd never held his breath under these conditions. Already his lungs felt as if they were about to burst. He didn't know how much longer he could last.

Then a strange thing happened—strange even for the Phantom. He was still clinging to the chain, his body going one way but his mind shooting off in another. In an instant, he cut through water, and then through rock and dirt, and he found himself, at least a part of himself, back in the pirate's chamber.

Why was he here?

"To witness the end," a voice said, and he sensed his father next to him.

The Phantom saw the pirates finally working their way free of the net. The ugly one with the scarred face slid down the mast and dropped to the floor. As soon as his feet touched down, a deep rumbling erupted somewhere beneath him. It grew louder and louder. The walls began to shake like a living thing in pain. Then a massive ball of fire burst into the pirates' chamber from the passageway connected to the torpedo chamber.

"Oh, oh!" the ugly pirate said, and that was all he said.

The ball of fire engulfed the chamber and ignited dozens of barrels of gunpowder. They exploded with such force that the cavern wall split open and the sea rushed in.

Nearly a mile away, the torpedo surfaced and

bobbed on calm waters. The Phantom broke the surface, too, and the moment he did, mind and body were united. He took in a deep gulp of air.

"Don't think I missed anything on this end," he said, and started swimming toward the floating torpedo. He worked his way along the torpedo to the panel. He unlocked it and slid the panel open.

"End of the line, ladies," he called down. "We swim from here."

Diana and Sala sat up, blinking against the bright daylight. Sala glanced slowly around, as though she couldn't quite believe they had made it and she was still alive. Diana threw her arms around the Phantom's neck.

In the distance, the fog-shrouded volcanic island was barely visible. Then the volcano erupted, spewing fire and debris high into the sky. The Phantom, Diana, and Sala watched in awe as the massive daytime fireworks display unfolded.

"Glad I'm not back there still," Sala said in a soft voice, then added: "Glad you guys aren't either."

Then a series of explosions blew off pieces of the island as if a great hammer wielded by a god were striking it. What remained—a craggy plain of dead rock and ash, fire and smoke—sank slowly beneath the waves.

"Look!" Diana pointed skyward.

The Sengh Brotherhood spider-web symbol appeared in the sky, formed by red smoke. Slowly it faded and dissolved, and as it did, the Phantom recalled the story of a boy who saw his father killed by pirates four hundred years ago and vowed to fight piracy.

Then his thoughts were interrupted as he saw an

enormous wall of water rolling their way. "A tidal wave," he shouted. "Move over, I'm getting in there."

"You can't, there's no room," Diana said.

"We'll just have to make room."

The three of them squeezed into the torpedo. It was a tight fit, but the Phantom somehow managed to slide the panel shut. And just in time. A massive wall of water slammed against the torpedo, picking it up as a thunderous roar surrounded them. They tumbled over and over in a wild, tumultuous explosion of movement. Then the torpedo began to rise and the waved lifted them up fifty feet or more until they rocketed along its crest.

Later, none of them would know exactly how long or how far they traveled on the wave. They were finally deposited on an inhabited island three hundred feet inland. Several kids pulled open the panel and ran when they saw the Phantom. No doubt a new legend of a strange sea monster was started that day on the island.

TWENTY-NINE

She felt as if she were living in a fairy tale as she listened to the Phantom tell his story in the Chronicle Room deep inside Skull Cave. They were sitting at a long table with a large leather-bound book open in front of them. Its yellowed pages, like all the books here, were filled with stories, all written in longhand.

Three months ago, Diana would not have believed that someone like the Phantom even existed. Masked heroes living in caves were characters from the world of fantasy. But now she not only believed it, she was hopelessly in love with this strange man.

After they had survived their escape from the Sengh Brotherhood's underground den, they'd found themselves on the remote Caribbean island of Providencia. Diana had wanted to return to Deep Woods with the Phantom, but he'd convinced her that she should go home and let her family know that she was all right. So she and Sala had hopped a ferry to the island of San Andres, returned to New York, and gone their own ways.

A few days later, a letter from the Phantom arrived

with a plane ticket to Bangalla enclosed. Diana had flown to Zavia and was met by Guran, who had escorted her into the jungle. After they'd crossed into Deep Woods, Devil had raced up to meet them, and then the Phantom had appeared atop Hero.

For the past three days, she and the Phantom had explored the forest and the beach, and her life had been idyllic. But she'd kept asking the Phantom to give her a better explanation of who he was. Finally this morning he had taken her into the Chronicle Room for the first time.

She frowned as the Phantom finished telling the tale of the little boy who had survived a massacre by pirates. "Over the decades and centuries, folks of the jungle, the city, and the sea began to whisper that there was a man who could not die, a phantom, a ghost who walks."

"That was a long time ago," she said. "You're not going to tell me that little boy was you, are you?"

"No. Of course not. How could that be? That would make me over four hundred years old." He closed the heavy book in which the first chronicles were recorded. "That boy became the first Phantom. I'm his descendant, Diana, and like him I pledged to carry out his oath to fight crime and piracy."

She looked at the skull ring on his finger. "But is that the same ring as the one the shaman gave the boy during the ceremony?"

"Yes, each boy who is to become the Phantom is given the skull ring at the age of sixteen. But he can't wear it until he really is the Phantom. Then he gives it to his first son when he reaches sixteen."

"So when your dad died, you put on the ring."

She thought a moment. "Does that mean all the Phantoms are killed before their sons take over?"

He shook his head. "No. Some, but not many, have survived their encounters with evil and turned over their mantle to their sons. Eventually they retired to this very chamber to write down their stories and the stories of their ancestors."

The Phantom picked up the gun belt that he'd recovered from Quill and walked over to a wall that was covered with weapons, some dating back four hundred years. "Twenty Phantoms came before me."

The Phantom hung his father's gun belt on the last peg. "I'm not immortal, Diana. I was born right here in this cave, and I was educated in America. When my father was killed, I came back to take his place."

Educated in America: that was just as she'd suspected. "And one day your own son will take your place, right?"

"Yes." The Phantom cleared his throat. He looked uncomfortable. But she pursued the matter, anyway.

"Where did all these Phantoms find their wives?" she asked.

He didn't hesitate to answer. "They found them in many places. One married a reigning queen, one a princess, another a beautiful red-haired barmaid. They all came back to live here in this strange, wonderful place."

"And did these wives know what he looked like?" she persisted.

"Yes, only the wife and their children could see his face."

A brief, awkward silence followed as Diana stared at him; she waited to see if he had anything further to say about the matter. Then Guran entered the room, taking the Phantom off the spot.

"The plane for Miss Palmer is waiting, Ghost Who Walks."

"Thank you, Guran," the Phantom said.

Guran nodded and left.

"Does Guran know the truth about you, that you're not immortal?"

"Oh, sure. He just likes to call me that." He paused. "Ghost Who Walks. It has kind of a nice ring to it."

Diana smiled, then bent down to ruffle Devil's fur. "Good-bye, Devil. Take good care of your master." She stood up, and looked at the Phantom. "I better go."

There was definitely something enjoyable about riding Hero with Diana in front of him, one hand on the reins, the other around her waist. He liked it, he decided. Liked it a lot. He didn't want her to leave Deep Woods, but he didn't want to push her into making a hasty decision, either. Life in the Bangalla jungle, after all, was a far cry from Diana's New York City. He wanted to give her time to think it over before he proposed anything to her.

He reined Hero to a halt and dismounted with Diana. "Where are we?" she asked.

"This way."

They took a few steps through the jungle, pushed through the lush tropical growth, and stopped at the top of a slope as the foliage gave way to a beautiful beach. Just offshore a seaplane was docked and a pilot, dressed in flight gear, stood on the beach, looking out to sea.

"Hey there!" the Phantom called.

The pilot turned and waved.

"It's Sala!" Diana shouted, and waved back.

"I guess I couldn't stay away," Sala yelled.

"I'll be right there," Diana called down to her.

Then she turned to the Phantom. He didn't know what to say to her. He didn't want any pledges of loyalty or promises of any kind. Not yet. Still, he wanted to make it clear to her how he felt and what he ultimately wanted.

"Before I go, take off your mask," Diana said. "Let me see your face . . . Kit."

So she knew, he thought. He had often wondered if she'd guessed. Turning his back to the beach, he pulled off the mask.

Diana smiled. "Hi, Kit."

"How long have you known?" he asked.

"Well, I suspected ever since New York when you, Kit, disappeared about the same time you, Phantom, arrived. But then there wasn't a whole lot of time to think about it, was there?"

"I guess not. You know, I'm not really permitted to reveal all these secrets, Diana."

"You're not?"

"Well, actually, I am. But to only one person," the Phantom explained.

"Who is that?"

"The woman I intend to marry."

"Oh, the woman you *intend* to marry?" Diana smiled. "But what if she refuses you?"

"Nobody refuses the Phantom."

"I suppose that's another one of those 'old jungle sayings.'"

"No. I just made it up."

She laughed and so did he.

Then he reached out, took her in his arms, and kissed her. It was a long, slow-building kiss that held the promise of much more to come. After they parted, they held each other's gaze for a long moment. Then Diana stepped away, still staring into the Phantom's unmasked eyes.

She turned and walked unsteadily down the slope toward the lagoon and the seaplane that would take her back to New York. The Phantom waited on the top of the slope as Diana and Sala paddled a raft out to the seaplane. He watched as they boarded the plane and then taxied away. As the seaplane took off, he replaced his mask and mounted Hero. He reined the stallion around and trotted back into the jungle.

As the seaplane skimmed over the treetops of the lush jungle, Sala turned to Diana and yelled over the sound of the roaring engine and the rushing wind. "Why don't you stay?"

"Uncle Dave and I have some unfinished business with the police commissioner."

She also had to get her life in order, to prepare for a long stay in a far-off place with the man she loved. She couldn't wait.

Sala nodded. "You'll be back."

Diana didn't reply, but she wore a wistful expression. Maybe in a month, she thought. If she could wait a month.

Maybe two weeks.

Sala pulled back on the yoke and the plane began to gain altitude. She tilted the right wing downward. "Look out your window, Diana!" Sala yelled.

The Phantom galloped to the top of a hill and was highlighted in the orange rays of the setting sun. Hero reared up on his hind legs as if to salute the departing plane. Then the Phantom rode off, disappearing into the jungle.